BEING CAREFREE IS FREEDOM

Janice A. Yehnert

ISBN 979-8-89309-399-5 (Paperback)
ISBN 979-8-89309-400-8 (Digital)

Covenant Books
11661 Hwy 707
Murrells Inlet, SC 29576
www.covenantbooks.com

DEDICATION

I dedicate this book to my four children (who are each unique in their own way), their children, my grandchildren, and my great-grandchildren. I hope with all my heart and soul that all of them will be able to grasp the truth about the one person who has not only given them life but has led them through life and provided blessings for them. That one person is Jesus Christ, the Son of God, God the Father, and the third part of the triune God, the Holy Spirit.

I want to thank all of my ancestors for giving to me the different characteristics that exist in my life. These people have inspired me to live life from the various forms of love that they bestowed upon me: my maternal grandmother (Thiebe-Hilger), my great-aunt (Helen Hilger), my mother (Emma Hilger), and my aunt (Parlie Hilger-Walborg); also, friends who have poured into my life not only values but morals and virtues that were part of the depths of their spirits. Some of these friends have been lifelong friends, while others were short-lived friendships for various reasons.

CONTENTS

FOREWORD

Here is my brief impression of the author's work of writing: Young people, you'll be surprised and enlightened when you grab hold of this story for a pole vault over the generation gap. Old people, this tantalizing, personal history will grab hold of you and your memory bank as it heartwarmingly portrays the hard work and continuous lessons of growing up in the midcentury Middle America. For those in the middle, who think you are too busy to read this book, your priorities probably need this adjustment.

Dr. Merrill D. Heim, EdD

ACKNOWLEDGMENTS

I would like to acknowledge and show my appreciation for the two mentors I had during my college degree programs: Missus Bea, who spent many hours critiquing my various term papers and assignments during my BA program while I attended Dakota Wesleyan University in South Dakota. She was a never-ending source of support and encouragement by providing the sense of having the candle (which I was burning at both ends) replaced. Missus Bea passed away in August of 1995 and was greatly missed (by her family and my family and myself) when I graduated from Dakota Wesleyan University in May of 1996. The other is Missus Lucinda, who was my number one fan and cheerleader combined together. She was my mentor during my pursuit of two master's degree programs at California State University of San Bernardino between the years of 2001 and 2006. Her positive attitude regarding my academic endeavors, hurdles, and future aspirations was uplifting to my spirit and motivated me to succeed.

I have changed the names of the people involved in my memoir to protect their privacy.

$$\mathcal{H}$$

BEING CAREFREE
IS FREEDOM

Those were the days of being young and free
From all that life hands out so frivolously
The cares, the burdens, the worries,
One needs not to embrace but buries
Until we reach the point of letting go.
Yet we take it on, as if we owe
It all and in our stead,
We all don't need
To go through life burdened down
But deserve and being honored with a crown,
Looking back to life carefree,
Free from worries, you see,
Having lived life with no regrets,
Causing us to possess few frets.
But rather, look at all that's well.
Therefore, catch the fragrant smell
Of life lived fully
Abundantly free, truly.
It's all a person could ask for
Dream and strive towards more
Of happiness and success
Thus, creating usefulness.

Janice A. Yehnert

CHAPTER 1

What Are Traditions

What can we say and comprehend about the subject of family traditions? What are traditions, and how do they get started in our lives in the first place? Traditions are defined as an inherited or established way of thinking put into action by someone who is courageous. They are relative to a person's culture, customs, and ethics. They form a birthright, an inheritance, and a legacy that can be carried throughout future generations. In the biblical sense of the definition, they are related to ancestral, immemorial, customary, habitual, and establishments that are fixed, common, and popular to individuals who have concern for such elements in their lives. For example, someone's great-grandfather believed in the Lord who lived a life according to the scriptures, which was very influential in his children's lives in the spiritual sense. Always going to church on Sundays and having the noon meal together as a family is a habitual, popular concern to the elements of their lives. Living a life of devotion to God and making sure family members did the same, not in the sense of religion but in the sense of having a heart for the things pertaining to God's command to live an obedient life according to scriptures of the Holy Bible. An ordinary family tradition can be passed down from generation to generation; this is actually an example that is contrary to what a tradition is in the spiritual sense. Spirituality cannot be passed down from generation to generation. Each individual has to make the choice of whether or not they will make their own commitment to the Lord Jesus Christ. Whether or not they will live their life according to God's Word and heed/follow the commandments of the Lord, it's up to the individual person of whether or not they will live a life that is up standing in the Lord's sight. Psalm 84:11 states, "No good thing will He withhold from those who walk uprightly."

Psalm 112:1–5 states, "Praise the Lord! Blessed is the man who fears the Lord, Who delights greatly in His commandments. His descendants will be knights on earth; the generation of the upright will be blessed. Wealth and riches will be in his house, and his righteousness endures forever. Unto the upright there arises light in the darkness; He is gracious, as well as being full of compassion, and righteous. A good man deals graciously and lends; He will guide his affairs with discretion," being "born again" with Jesus and choosing to accept Him into their hearts, living for Him, sacrificing all worldly thoughts and gains to follow Jesus (Romans 3:21–26; Luke 18:17; John 3:3–4).

Everyone has some family traditions. It's interesting to investigate and discover who started them and why they started the traditions that we have in our ancestral backgrounds. If we want to do this, we will have to ask the older generations before us how certain traditions began. But some may ask the question, why are traditions even necessary? Family traditions are necessary when an individual desires to leave a legacy for his/her children and grandchildren. In our family, we have many family traditions, and they have provided comfort and joy in generations before us. But they may create provoking thoughts for the individuals in the younger generations who now live.

Traditions are existent in our families because our ancestors (especially mothers and grandmothers) wanted to live and expound rich, wholesome lives to their children and grandchildren. I believe that my European ancestors started traditions in order to form loving memories of our childhood days and to create traditions; they then also lived more rich, carefree lives even though, financially, their lives were not always so rich.

✤

CHAPTER 2

Early 1900s

My dad used to tell stories about the dirty thirties, during the depression years, the gas rations, and the lack of useful, essential resources. Let's face it, in the dirty thirties, there wasn't much going on that was worth holding on to for financial gain. The stock markets crashed, which is part of having a depression in the country. "In the beginning of the 1930s, more than fifteen million Americans—fully one-quarter of all wage-earning workers—were unemployed. *J. Edgar Hoover was president of the United States at that time, and he really did not know what to do with everything that was taking place at the time. He didn't think that solving such problems was really the federal government's job, and he thought that the behavior of Wall Street speculators had contributed in a significant way to the crisis. American people needed help to survive in those times, and it didn't look like President J. Edgar Hoover was going to help the American people out of their dilemma. He was the long-time director of the FBI (1924–1972) and spent much of his career, before becoming president of the United States, gathering intelligence on radical groups and individuals and subversives, Martin Luther King Jr. being one of his favorite targets. Hoover's methods included infiltration, burglaries, illegal wiretaps, and planted evidence, and his legacy is tainted because of it. He died in Washington, DC, on May 2, 1972.*

In 1932, Franklin Delano Roosevelt was elected president of the United States. In the first nine years, Roosevelt created the new deal, which was a new role for government in American life. By June of the first year after he was elected, President Roosevelt and the congress had passed fifteen major laws—including the Agricultural Adjustment Act, the Glass-Steagall Banking Bill, the Home Owners Loan Act, the Tennessee Valley Authority Act, and the National Industrial Recovery Act—that fundamentally reshaped many aspects of the American economy. As Roosevelt had declared in his inaugural address, "the only thing we have to fear is fear itself." He also "shored up the nation's banks" to keep the enemy out of the United States territory. He served twelve years as president of the United States until his death in 1945.

Between 1930 and 1933 over nine thousand banks closed in the US, which took $2.5 billion in deposits. Meanwhile, people did what they could do, and that was stand in charity lines and sell fruit on the street corners to bring in moneys for their families.

The Great Plains states were considered a dust bowl, especially the states of Kansas, Oklahoma, and parts of Texas. And there were grasshoppers that brought ruin to the Midwest states of Iowa, Nebraska, and South Dakota. In the summer of 1931, a swarm of grasshoppers descended on crops throughout the American heartland, devastating millions of acres in those three states mentioned. This happened in the midst of a bad drought, and people suffered tremendously from this disaster.

Since the Midwest was already experiencing a heavy drought, the environment created friendly conditions for grasshoppers and locusts to deposit their egg pods in the soil that was available to them. Since the very beginning of agriculture, people had struggled to prevent insects from eating their crops. With the drought conditions, the people had no chance of warding off the insects that came and laid their egg pods in the soil.

The locusts and grasshoppers would travel in swarms, and they hit up against your body and clung against your clothing. "These insects undergo a significant transformation when they become part of a swarm. Their wings and jaws grow, enabling them to travel greater distances and increasing their appetite" (History.com).

"In 1931, a swarm of locusts or grasshoppers were said to be so thick that it blocked out the sun, and one could shovel the grasshoppers with a scoop. Cornstalks were eaten to the ground and fields left completely bare. Since the early 1930s, swarms have not been seen in the United States. However, North Africa and parts of the Middle East continue to experience problems with insect swarms, which sometimes include as many as one billion bugs" (History.com).

One great thing that was accomplished back in the 1930s was the establishment of the Social Security Act and its regulations. "Responding to the economic impact of the Great Depression, five million old people in the early 1930s joined nationwide Townsend clubs, promoted by Francis E. Townsend, to support his program demanding a $200 monthly pension for everyone over the age of sixty. In 1934, Pres. Franklin D. Roosevelt set up a committee on economic security to consider the matter; after studying its recommendations, Congress in 1935 enacted the Social Security Act, providing old-age benefits to be financed by a payroll tax on employers and employees. Railroad employees were covered separately under the Railroad Retirement Act of 1934. The Social Security Act has been periodically amended, expanding the types of coverage, bringing progressively more workers into the system, and adjusting both taxes and benefits in an attempt to keep pace with inflation" (Encyclopedia Britannica, Inc.).

"By the end of the 1930s, the New Deal had come to an end. Growing congressional opposition made it difficult for President Roosevelt to introduce new programs. At the same time, as the threat of war loomed on the horizon, the president turned his attention away from domestic politics. In December 1941, the Japanese bombed Pearl Harbor, and the US entered World War II. The war effort stimulated American industry, and the Great Depression was over."

Three of my maternal uncles served in World War II and the Korean War. The fourth uncle served in the navy and was a cook aboard one of the naval carriers. Both my mom's parents and my dad's parents were farmers. My mom and her sister, Sally, worked out in the field, as if they were men. My mom talked about how she missed her brothers when they were far away in another country, fighting for the U.S. people's freedom. "They would write home to my sisters and parents," my mom used to tell me. Farmers in the Midwestern states were playing a Russian roulette game (gambling) when they placed their seed crop into the soil. My dad would tell me, "I always hoped for a good, abundant crop and that rain and moisture would not be scarce that year. This created faith and hope in my heart that those farmers put their sweat and tears into the whole process."

Mom told how her mother, Grandma Theibe, sewed all of their clothes, including undergarments. She went on to say, "Everything from heavy winter coats to petticoats and bloomers (underskirts and underpants) got sewn from Grandma's treadle sewing machine that was run by the feet moving a big metal open designed apparatus that was located by the floor." Grandma Thiebe passed down the art of sewing to my mom, and my mom passed it down to us children.

I took sewing in home economics class during high school, and I'm sure that my sister Victoria did the same. I also passed down the art of sewing to my children. I did the same thing that my mom taught me how to do. When the children turned eight to ten years old, they practiced mending clothes and then went on to things that they were interested in sewing. My two younger children learned how to sew quilts when they attended the Christian school during the 1990s.

In the 1940s, there were all sorts of people trying to make a living financially. I don't think that the hobos and gypsies took much responsibility in making a living in those days for themselves. It seemed that they didn't take much pride in earning their own way through life but took the easy way out and begged from other people, who were trying to make a living for themselves.

I heard a story from a client of mine about how some people opted to ride trains as what we call hobos in the forties. He said, "Women were also in this category." They also returned home and were able to get jobs. Their families weren't crazy about the fact that their loved ones were risking their lives to live the life as a hobo, but eventually those people settled down into regular jobs around the

World War II era. Sanford also told me, "There was an organization called the community civilian camp (CCC) that put the men to work either building houses, building railroads, or clearing off woodlands for the lumber." He went on to tell his story that "these camps were located in different states" Most of these men went on from there to get college educations and steady professional jobs."

My mom would tell stories about the hobos or gypsies and how they would come and ask her mom for a live chicken, and they would work some for them. Grandma never wanted those people around her farm, so she would just give them a chicken and a fresh loaf of bread, then they would be on their way. My mom would tell how the children all stood behind Grandma's apron for protection. They were skeptical of the strangers and gypsies that would travel around to their farm and other neighbors' farms as well.

Although none of the deals that President Roosevelt put into place in the government brought the depression to an end, people still did not have much money to spare. But people had radios, and listening to the radio was free. There were popular broadcasts that could be listened to by the people, and these programs acted as an object that distracted people from their everyday struggles. I remember Jack Benny and a couple of Western programs that were broadcasted in the mid-1950s. And there were the other comedy programs, like Amos 'n' Andy; soap operas; and sporting events, such as boxing matches.

Swing music encouraged people to cast aside their troubles and dance. Bandleaders, like Benny Goodman and Fletcher Henderson, drew crowds of young people to ballrooms and dance halls around the country.

I can remember in the 1960s when my parents took my siblings and myself to a ballroom in Norfolk, where the jazz bands would come to entertain on Saturday nights. My parents would invite several other couples to join us for the evening, and we learned how to ballroom dance. Some of the dances that were popular then were the cha-cha, waltz, the foxtrot, and the two-step. People found pleasure where they could in those days. During the weekdays, they experienced working hard in the fields or with household chores.

Sometimes food was scarce on the farm, but usually butchering time would take place in the fall, which provided enough meat for a year. When food was put on the table, it was sometimes measured meal by meal, most of the time without the presence of meat, maybe the existence of just the staples of bread or a potato and maybe one vegetable to partake of that particular sitting down to eat. The adult women in the family grew huge gardens in order to preserve those foods grown into glass jars. Those food-filled jars were stored in a deep cave or a basement, if one existed. A lot of families who owned their property would dig a deep cave that was at least twelve feet below the ground surface. This was essential in order to provide a cool, dark place to store the jars of preserved foods. If canned foods are stored in a warm climate, the seals of the jars would come loose, and the food would spoil. All the hard work of canning the foods would be lost. Wooden steps would be built down into the cave in order to get up and down out of it with the jars of food.

Some homes had a dumbwaiter, which consisted of metal shelves that were welded together to hold food, such as cream, milk, cheese, butter, and other articles desired to be kept cold. This series of shelves were attached to a chain or rope to pull the articles that were placed on it to the top out of a cylinder-shaped hole in the kitchen pantry.

Then as the years went by, World War II was over, and the 1950s came into being when the baby boomers were born. Joy was again being restored. Life was easing up a little financially for the parents of these babies who were being born. The elements that were needed to create and embrace wealth and freedom, such as gasoline and electricity, were being made plentiful. Then the inventions took place with modern automobiles, more modern tractors, and farm equipment. Then electric washers were replacing the gas-operated washers for clothes. Also, the invention of telephones increased the possibility to communicate with neighbors and loved ones. Other useful items were invented to help ease the labor of people in order to get the job done quicker: electric food mixers, electric meat grinders, clothes dryers that were run by electricity. All these devices would provide the housewives with more time to devote to their husbands and children.

It was also the restoration period regarding the spiritual aspect in these people's lives. They were freer when they went to church by being able to more readily pay their tithes (10 percent of their earnings) to the church. The spiritual principles that were true were being put into place in the preachers' sermons. Once again, they worshipped the one true, living Savior, who had brought them through all the tough times. The one resource was God, "who is the same yesterday, today, and forever." People were being enlightened about the only one Savior who still could and was providing for their every need on a daily basis. So traditions came into being to add some spark into the lives of not only their children and children's children but to their own for part of the survival solution.

CHAPTER 3

Family Traditions

There were many traditions that were started as far back as the early 1900s in our mother's family, the Hilgers' side of the family. Most of them did add a spark of life, a twinkle in the eye, a leap in the heart, a satisfaction in the soul of people who were among the mom and siblings, the family members from generation to generation. The frequent occurrences of family gatherings and the family gatherings for the various holidays were delightful to attend. Along with these family gatherings came the fun event of dressing up with straw hats for all of the girl cousins and having their picture taken together.

Another time, it was all the girl cousins wore the same color of dresses. It was a proud tradition for mothers to sew dresses out of the same kind of material for themselves and their daughters. I remember that my mom sewed us many matching sets of dresses, and she also did this for my two older sisters, Flossie and Victoria. We all were so proud of the matching dresses that we could wear to church and special occasions.

There was a favorite aunt of every individual in our family; her name was Parlie, short for Pearl Rose. That was her nickname from early on in life. Her given name when she was born was Pearl Rose, and she was the youngest daughter in the family. She was the one with the camera in hand (shutter bug) during the family gatherings. She also made homemade root beer soda and bottled that potion into small bottles that held no more than a cup and a fourth of the drink. We were allowed two bottles of that wonderful tasting soda, only on the day of each family gathering. Otherwise, it sat in the spare refrigerator in Aunt Parlie's basement until the next gathering occurred.

Sometimes there was the homemade ice cream. The taste of the rich, creamy, cold, sweet substance of homemade ice cream on a person's tongue and in the mouth on a hot summer day was delicious. We usually ate until our stomachs could hold no more ice cream. And every month, we would gather together, either at my maternal grandmother's house or at one of the other aunt and uncle's house, and each person who had a birthday that month would get their very own birthday cake. There would be an angel food cake, a chocolate cake with rich creamy chocolate frosting, a yellow lemon cake with thick white creamy frosting, and a scoop of ice cream to nestle up against the slice of cake, adding its sweet, creamy taste to that of the cake.

We also had this spiritual tradition according to the holy sacraments of the Lutheran Church that when each baby was baptized by sprinkling in a Sunday morning service, where all the relatives attended the event, then godparents of the baby were chosen by the parents of the baby. So when we had the monthly birthday celebrations that female or couple godparents of the baby would make a special cake for that godbaby's birthday. It didn't matter how old the godchild became; they still got a cake made just for them. Gifts were also given to the person with the birthday from not only the godparents but by other relatives as well.

I have to include the holiday of Christmas with the Hilger family, my mom's side of the family. Everyone seemed to be determined to have the family gatherings. Because it was always cold weather, let alone weather that produced snow in December for Christmastime. But the aunts and uncles from Omaha and surrounding towns all made it to Grandma's house for the occasion. The cousins would line up on the stairsteps to get pictures taken. I remember the one year when all the younger grandchildren received teddy bears with squeakers in their stomachs. I didn't have mine for a very long time. and Jake, my brother, took it from my arms and threw it on the floor and stomped on my teddy bear's stomach until he broke the squeaker. I was so disappointed of his actions that it made me cry at the time. It seemed like he had an inner temper to begin with in life. Maybe he was angry because he didn't have a brother to play with but an older sister who forced him to play with dolls, etc. But for the most part, Christmas was an occasion that was happy to be remembered, sharing them with my cousins.

Then there was the tradition of sending the daughters to live with the maternal grandmother for various reasons. There existed the generational tradition of the girls wearing long hair until they reached a certain age. That age was around eight years old. And the not so fun tradition of all was that one of having the girls helping with household duties at a very young age. The young girls were led to believe that having the opportunity of helping with the daily household duties was because they had the little hands and fingers that were necessary to get the job done. But this tradition did have a long-lasting effect on the young girl's life. Having this weekly or daily household task taught the young girl work ethics that she would need later in life.

We all wonder why traditions have stopped in our generation. Even the baby boomers have stopped the traditions of the last generational ancestors. The main reason why the traditions have stopped is warranted to the new methods of this generation. The freedom to move wherever a job that suits a person exists, the freedom of moving to the kind of climate that a person desires to live in, the freedom to move 1,800 miles (physical distance) from the older generation, and the newer generation have separated physically from their relatives to the degree that they are no longer able to keep the family traditions alive.

The next generation, we have labeled the people of this generation the x generation. They don't seem to have the same family values that the baby boomers have had in the past years. They live too busy of lives. About 20 percent of the x generation embraces family reunions. Some of these people are not interested in what others are saying or doing. There are those who could care less about where their inheritance, culture, or ethnic group has come from. (Their roots are not important to them.) They desire to do things their own way. And most of those people are not serving the Lord in their lives, so they have a different perception of life. Also, how they should live their lives is dependent upon how they were raised rather than what the biblical version advises on how to treat your spouse, how to raise your children, how to treat your neighbor (positive or negative). Some just want to do their own thing, and they are not open to the advice of others.

Computers, telephones, and cell phones are helping to replace seeing relatives in person physically. Values and views on respecting people, who are older than oneself, have changed in some families. People have become selfish and self-centered; thus they don't want to share their busy lives with older people. Some don't value the family unit any longer, yet many wonder why they don't have the blessings that they desire in life, or they cannot and will not recognize the blessings that they do have in their lives.

❆

CHAPTER 4

Life in 1950s and 1960s

Let us go back in time to the early 1950s, and take a look at what life was like for me, Janice, born to a sharecrop farmer, Helmer and his wife, Emma. I was born in August of 1950, the third-born sibling to two sisters. My older sister Flossie was ten years my senior and my other sister Victoria was seven years my senior in age. Hopefully, some light will be shed on what life was like in those years when time did not vanish so quickly. I desire to share with you what traditions were present in my life and what traditions I chose to keep in my life that bring satisfaction and peace to my life as well.

With the many unseen blessings in life, I lived what seemed a normal life. I had loving parents, who worked hard to make a living as sharecroppers in the Midwest state of Nebraska. These same loving parents made many mistakes in their choices throughout their lives, but nevertheless, they still loved their children. When I was born, my parents lived by Platte Center. Helmer farmed the same land that his dad, Delmar, did until his mother, Emily, went to live in the town of Columbus, Nebraska. After this event happened, we moved to Lindsay and lived there for eight years. I had two older sisters, Flossie and Victoria, and a younger brother, Jake, who was three years younger than me. The Lindsay farm place was called the Polzen place because the landlady's last name was Polzen. We named the places where we lived by the last name of the owner of that place.

At the age of five, I played with my baby dolls and pretended I was a mommy. I never could figure out why my mom gave me a black baby doll one year for Christmas. I don't know why I didn't ask her why she gave it to me, but I didn't. The most prominent feature I dreamed about was showing love to my own babies someday. I watched my mom and her mom's friends take care of their babies and knew in my heart that someday I would be like them and be a good mother to babies of my own. It was while sitting on those tall cement steps on the backside of the A-framed, white farmhouse that was located by Lindsay that my longings turned into dreams. That was my home at that time, and there was a caring, nurturing character in me that began to grow.

Living in rural Nebraska had its advantages and disadvantages. Along with the rural life that I experienced was the existence of rural school houses. The first school that I attended was located three miles from my home in the country. It consisted of one room with a built-in porch, where snow boots were removed and stored during school hours, and coats were hung on hooks to dry from the wetness of the snow. The building did not have a basement to it, and the teacher's desk sat in the front of the room with the large blackboards hanging on the wall behind the desk. The schools in the fifties were named after what district they were in at that time.

My siblings and I attended District 18, which consisted of one teacher, who taught kindergarten through eighth grade with the class size each being usually two or three students. In this particular school, there were approximately a total of fifteen or eighteen children who attended District 18. My first teacher was Mrs. Hort when I was in kindergarten. I had her as a teacher for one year before Mrs. Simmon came to be the teacher. Mrs. Hort was younger than Mrs. Simmon and seemed to have less patience with the students learning what they needed to learn than Mrs. Simmon. Mrs. Hort had only one daughter, in comparison to Mrs. Simmon, who had raised two boys. Mrs. Hort told Emma, my mom, that she did not place high hopes for me, according to my academic scores that year. That was the year that I struggled with being sick quite frequently (over half of the school year) with tonsillitis. I eventually had my tonsils removed when I turned five years old.

When Mrs. Simmon became my teacher, she had a different approach to not only me but toward all of the students who attended that school. The students heard a lot of positive affirmations from Mrs. Simmon, and I recall that the students had more positive attitudes toward one another and toward themselves and their academic achievements. As I recall, Mrs. Simmon's attitude made a definite positive impact on my life. It seemed that I was able to understand and remember what I was taught, and I took an interest in reading at an early age.

One thing that I will never forget in my mind is that Mrs. Simmon and her husband were there early each day when school was to be in session and had the schoolhouse warm for the students when they arrived. In the middle of the one-room schoolhouse stood an oil-burner stove that kept the inside of the building warm in the wintertime.

Mr. Simmon was a very small-statured person, but he had the bluest eyes you ever could imagine, which contrasted with his gray, silvery-colored hair. And his grin was shiny that made a person smile back at him. Mrs. Simmon stood taller than her husband, wore glasses and had this full head of graying hair. She was a little larger in stature and always radiated the attitude that everyone was somebody special. Her words and character expounded that this was a fact, not just a fleeting thought.

All the students who attended that school played well with each other, and there was an underlying respect for one another. Although there was one student, Kimball, who, for one reason or another, did not like girls who played with dolls at school. The girls who brought dolls to school were the Neilson sisters. The dolls that they brought to school fit into a medium-sized pillbox purse. They included extra changes of dresses for the dolls, and everything was stashed into that black-colored pillbox purse, with rhinestones along the edge of the flat lid. Kimball got this mischievous idea to take the purse away from the girls and hide it from them until the last recess was over for the day. It seemed that no one ever knew that it was gone because no one asked any questions about it. I grew tired of watching him do this escapade every week and finally told Kimball that if he did it again, he would be doing it without me helping him. I also included the statement that if he did it again with me knowing it, I would be tempted to tell the teacher about what he was doing.

Kimball was always getting himself into trouble after that. It seemed that since he didn't get caught doing his escapade involving the purse that he thought no one would catch him doing anything that was wrong. It wasn't long after that incident that he got caught writing on the outside of one of the outhouses with a black crayon. I don't remember what words he wrote, but Mrs. Simmon had him scrub the words off the outside boards of the outhouse with a pan of water and Comet cleanser. I remember noticing that his little, chubby hands were beet red in color because it was chilly out that day when this incident happened to take place. He was saying all kinds of uncanny words as he proceeded to scrub those words off that out-house. I didn't have time to encourage mischievous tricks since I had my own wholesome goals and expectations for my life. And besides all that about Kimball, his fingers were always stinky, like snails. He had a lot of aquariums with snails in them at his home. I don't know why he raised snails. I never did ask him why he did that. Maybe he sold them to people who liked to go fishing with them as bait; I don't really know why for sure.

By the time I was seven, I had a burning desire to play the piano. I begged my mom to let me take piano lessons. "Please let me take piano lessons," I would beg of her. At the age of eight, I started beginner's piano lessons. My piano teacher was a spinster, who lived with her parents in Newman Grove. In one short year, I stopped my lessons with the lady, Miss T., because I wasn't learning much from Miss T., and she had an odious disposition about her. So I self-taught the notes that I had not learned from Miss T. and practiced until I thought I was ready to restart lessons with another piano teacher.

When I was thirteen, I started piano lessons with a lovely lady, Mrs. P., who heartily praised me as her student to try harder and succeed at learning the piano. The whole event was successful, and I learned quickly how to play classical music and enjoyed learning from Mrs. P. Thus, I continued to take lessons for two or three years and, later in life, as an adult, used my musical talent to play piano in several of the churches that I attended. Music brought much joy into my life and into the lives of others as they heard me not only playing a tune but also singing along with the tune. My mom and I spent many hours singing to the playing on the big upright piano that was located in the living room of our home by Newman Grove. We called that farmplace the Noreen place because the people who lived there before that time had the last name of Noreen.

My siblings and I did not have many friends in our elementary school years. We shared a friendship with the neighborhood family, who lived down the road about three miles from the Polzen house, where we lived then. They had two children, Lydia and Jerry. Lydia was three years younger than my sister, Victoria, and two years older than me. The years until I got to high school age, Lydia was Victoria's friend, and then she became my friend after Victoria graduated from high school. Jerry was three years younger than me. When he was eight, and I was eleven, he and I became infatuated with each other. We just liked to hug each other. I never will forget that he bought this ring for me that had a great big purple stone in it. I wouldn't wash my hands with it on because I didn't want to ruin it. He kept it a secret from Lydia that he had given me the ring. I didn't always wear it either because I didn't know how my mom would react to him giving me the ring. It was a secret that we tried to keep between us. We had my sister take a picture of us standing, hugging each other by the side with our heads together. A special memory that I hold dearly is that, every once in a while, for no reason at all, he would kiss me on the cheek quickly. He was really a sweet boy, and at the time, I thought that he was wistfully cute.

Lydia and Jerry, on occasion, would ride their big bay-colored horse, Ginger, down the road to visit my siblings and me. We would ride Ginger down into the canyons that were part of the land that my dad rented. Riding horses in the canyons was always a peaceful experience for all of us. We created an order of getting on the horse, Ginger, and stuck to this order every time because it worked well for us. Jake was the littlest, so he would ride in front of the saddle. Lydia would take her place in the saddle because she was the driver of the horse. Next, Victoria would ride immediately behind the saddle, with me following next in line. And Jerry would take up the rear, which ended to be on the very top of the horse's tail. Jerry was a tough little boy at the age of eight. He had some huskiness to him, if you know what I mean. He definitely had to do some creative maneuvers in order to stay on board Ginger while riding up and down through the canyons.

Ginger was a long-bodied horse, and her gait was slow and smooth. She stood quietly while all her passengers climbed aboard her into their designated places. The trips that they made lasted around two hours, if not longer. When the trip was done, and we arrived back at our home, Mom usually had some hot home-baked pastry and a cool pitcher of Kool-Aid awaiting the hungry, tired crew of youngsters. We would devour the freshly baked goodies, usually homemade cinnamon rolls, or fresh, hot buns and butter. We would drink the cold, refreshing drinks with much gusto while we discussed how the trip in the canyons had been that time. Lydia always expressed her gratefulness to Emma for the delicious food. Jerry was thankful for the cold drink.

Another good memory that sticks in my mind is shaking mulberries. We had a mulberry tree out in the grove, just north of the house on the Noreen place. Mom would take an old, white sheet designated for mulberry shaking because it was all stained from the purple hue of the mulberries juice. She would tie one corner of the sheet onto a lower branch and have two of us kids hold onto another corner each, and then she would take the garden rake and attach it to another low branch and shake that branch. When she did this, the mulberries would fall off into the middle of the white sheet. The sheet would become the color of the mulberries. It became a beautiful purple-blue color. We would do this procedure over and over again until Mom had enough mulberries to suit her fancy. It usually amounted to a full big milk bucket of mulberries. She would take them back to the house and pour out a full strainer at a time, wash and separate them, and fix us each a bowl full of fruits, served with milk and sugar on top. Then she would take the rest, freeze some in little bags that she put into little freezer boxes, and then leave some to make mulberry pies with the addition of strawberries. Mulberry pie was delicious with a small scoop of vanilla ice cream on top of it!

Summers were great in our young lives! We didn't have much, but we really didn't compare our materialistic possessions to other kids either. Mom made sure that she took us to the public swimming pool in our small hometown. We were raised in the country, and town was ten miles away from our home. Our small town, Newman Grove, consisted of 180 people, at least the sign stated, outside the city limits. In town, there was the high school and elementary school for the town kids. Actually, the schools served at least three or four different towns. There was the fire station, the city library, a photography shop, two grocery stores, the post office, a dime store, a drugstore, a creamery, a bowling alley, a theater, a doctor, a community hospital, and approximately six or seven churches. The fire station's size was adequate for the sixties. I visited the city library a lot during the summer months. I spent a lot of time reading books to pass the long hours when I was not working in the garden or fields, cleaning house, or ironing clothes. I read the whole *Hardy Boys* series, Laura Ingalls Wilder books, and other stories about kids that were popular in those days. We weren't allowed to watch television, so we filled the time with reading books and sometimes playing board games with our mom.

Newman Grove was a very interesting small town. I found that the photography shop was the most interesting place while observing the various pictures that were on display. It was owned by the Olson sisters. The one sister, Ethel, was short and petite, and the other sister, Erma, was taller and heavier set in stature. Erma was jollier in character than Ethel. Later in life, we discovered that the sisters were aunts to Marie, who became my brother's wife. They were her mother's sisters.

The grocery stores differed in character. Since Newman Grove was at least an hour away from a large town, where a person could buy gloves, jewelry, and such items that were necessary. It was necessary for one of the grocery stores to carry such items. The store had a heavy large door that you pulled open to enter into it. When a person got into the general store, you were surrounded by bolts of material for sewing garments, racks of clothes, glass showcases of jewelry, and countertops full of socks, gloves, undergarments, and so on. As a child, this all was sometimes overwhelming to me. Everything was so high above my head, and I couldn't see anything but all these items mentioned. Then at the far end of the general store were grocery items that were for sale.

The other grocery store, The Burnes' Market, sold strictly food items. They had a meat counter in the back of the store. There was the smell of fresh meat and the blood from the meat in the air. If you held your breath for a little while and took in small amounts of the smell at a time, a person could eventually get used to the pungent smell. You could get your fresh meat there, whether it would be ground beef, roast beef, chicken, pork cuts, or lunch meats. Lunch meats were a delicacy for sandwiches that were made for lunchtime every weekday. My mom would tell the man behind the counter how much she wanted of the lunch meat, how thick she wanted it sliced, and he would slice it and weigh it for her. It was placed on a piece of thin paper and then placed on a piece of thick butcher paper, wrapped up a certain way and taped. It was marked with a crayon marker of the price Emma had to pay for that item.

When a person walked into the dime store, you walked right into a counter of different compartments that held at least twelve varieties of candies. The next thing a person had to do was decide what candy and how much of it that you wanted to purchase. The varieties varied from chocolate-covered raisins to chocolate-covered peanuts to gum drops. A person could purchase as little as a dime's worth of chocolate-covered raisins or any of the variety of other candies offered there. You would tell Mr. Burton, the owner of the store, what you wanted and how much, and he would measure out to the penny any kind of candy that you desired to eat. He had a special scale that had a removable pan on top that was the shape of a kidney, where he poured the candies into with a scoop out of the candy's glass compartment. I always bought a dime's worth of chocolate-covered raisins. They tasted oh so good! The rest of the store had cosmetics and all the essentials that women need to get through the month and life.

The drugstore not only had the pharmacy but also was quite modern for its era. It also carried its own supply of cosmetics, rubbing alcohol, sterile items, hydrogen peroxide, and bandages. And of course, people of the town and surrounding towns would get their prescriptions filled there. Mr. Wilburn, I believe, was the owner of the pharmacy.

There was the creamery, where people from the country sold the cream from milking the cows and eggs that were collected from the chickens. Different varieties of cheeses were processed at the creamery and cream, milk, and eggs were available for the town people to purchase.

The eggs that were collected from the chickens on our farm were sold at a grocery store in another town that we lived by at that time. Lindsay was a much smaller town than Newman Grove. Its population was sixty in the best years. There was just one grocery store that sold garden tools, clothing, and food. It was a combination of food store and department store. Not much else existed in that town but the post office. On Wednesday nights, in the summertime, we all went to the free open-air movies. The long two-by six-boards were balanced on cement blocks that provided the seats that were sat on during the movies. The popcorn guy would pop the corn in his machine on the sidewalk behind, where we sat to watch the movie. Popcorn was ten cents a paper bag, and soda pop was fifteen cents a twelve-ounce bottle. My siblings and I were given enough money for one of each item to eat and drink during the movies. When the carnival came to town, more people came to town. The main street of Lindsay consisted of one long block, so it became very congested when the carnival was in town during the summer.

When Halloween would roll around on the calendar of events, Lydia and Jerry would accept the invitation of coming over to our house and enjoy the festivities of bobbing for apples and eating homemade popcorn balls. Bobbing for apples was a fun event. Mom would fill a washtub with water and place six apples in the water. The apples would float on top of the water and would bob around in the water. It was like the apples were enticing us to catch them as we could. But in order to capture an apple in the water, we had to put our faces underwater, open our mouths wide, and bite into the apple under the water. Our faces and sometimes our heads would be dripping wet after we were done bobbling for those apples. A towel would be provided for each of us after we caught the apple in the water and bit into the apple. We couldn't use our hands to help catch the apple, so the top of our heads would go deep into the water to actually catch the apple and bring it up to the surface of the water.

After bobbing for apples, we would get dressed up like hobos, clowns, or fancy ladies and go trick-or-treating in our small town, Newman Grove. People in town would recognize us and would have us introduce ourselves to them, just for common courtesy. Everyone could trust everyone else in those days, and so caramel apples, homemade popcorn balls, and other homemade goodies were readily handed out. All the goodies for the night were collected in the white pillowcases that were used for that purpose. The goodies that were cherished the most were the large chocolate bars, the caramel apples, and the bubblegum. Bubblegum was a new commodity in those days, and the children had a thirsty taste bud for it. When we arrived back home, we would dump our pillowcases on the floor or on the kitchen table and sort out the different candies that we had gathered during the evening. Sharing our candies was very present in our household; being stingy was not allowed. Considering sharing with other people was an unspoken element that was present.

Enjoying people brought the pleasure of family unions. Family reunions were always fun for me. Most of the family reunions were held in the big park in Columbus. It was fun there because of the presence of swings, slippery slides, and teeter-totters to play on and pass the time away. One year, we were visited by Great-Uncle Henry, the Lutheran preacher from Missouri, at our home by Lindsay. We lived on the Polzen place at that time.

Those cousins in Missouri believed differently than we did because they were brought up in the Missouri Synod Lutheran Church. We were brought up in the American Lutheran Synod

Church's beliefs. They had a different belief of how a person gets to go to heaven when they die.

Since I have become a Christian and now attend Full Gospel churches, I believe in what the whole Bible tells how to live out our lives. I'll tell you my version/perception of the difference in beliefs of how you get to heaven when you die by the knowledge and experience that I have gained in my own life. The Missouri Synod Lutherans believe that you dedicate your baby to the Lord because, as a baby, a person cannot make that decision for themselves at that young age. Samuel and Jesus were dedicated as babies in the temple to the Lord by their parents who lived in biblical times. They also believe that a person has to make a personal commitment to Jesus and live for Him—obey His commandments when you are at an accountable age—around eleven or twelve years old. At the time that this happens, a person acknowledges Jesus as their Lord and Savior and that Jesus died on the cross for their sins. They invite Jesus to live in their heart/life and for His direction in their life. The scriptures, in the book of Romans, also state that each one of us will stand before the Lord when we die and personally be held accountable for our own life. These people pray every day to Jesus and talk to Him, as if He was actually a person walking with them on earth, in the mindset of talking with a spiritual Heavenly Father. And they also ask that Jesus would guide them through the rest of their life. And Jesus reassures us that He will provide guidance for us here on earth because He says in His scriptures that the Holy Spirit is in each of us after we have committed our life to Him to be our guide. If you fail to obey God, you say a personal confession to God in private. And through His mercy and grace—according to the Holy Bible's scriptures—He is faithful to forgive you of your sins that you have committed. And you go on in life and ask God to help you not to sin, with God's help, in that area of your life because each one of us are at an age of accountability to recognize what is the right and wrong thing to do in all circumstances in life. And after making a commitment to Jesus, we now have the desire to do what is right in the decisions that we make in situations we encounter in life. We stay reading the Bible for answers and guidance in living our lives holy and acceptable to

God. The Wisconsin Synod Lutherans believe the same principles as the Missouri Synod Lutherans.

The American Lutherans, on the other hand, believe that you must go through and complete all the sacraments—baptism as a baby, with godparents taking on the responsibility of helping to teach the child about Jesus. They are supposed to help the parents raise up the child as a God-fearing person throughout their life. This comes by attending and completing confirmation and getting confirmed, which gives you the right of passage to take communion. If you have attended to all of the sacraments of the Lutheran Church, you are now on your way to heaven when you die. This also means that you can live your life the way you see fit. You can drink alcohol, indulge in drugs, use curse words, lie or steal from other people, and basically, the mercy and grace of God will carry you through life.

Uncle Henry came to visit with his Bible in his hand and the love of Jesus that he shed among everyone. He was a walking testimony of how Jesus is in personality Himself. Peter, in the scripture (1 Peter 2:3–5), talked about him: "Come and, like living stones be yourselves built into a spiritual house, for a holy dedicated priesthood, to offer up spiritual sacrifices that are acceptable and pleasing to God." He visited our family only when we lived in the big A-framed, white house by Lindsay. The Polzen house had a large, two-roomed parlor and a large living room. There was more than adequate amount of room for all of the relatives to sit and be comfortable in those rooms. After that occasion, it seemed that he could not travel the distance any longer to visit the relatives in the Midwest. I always felt a peace come upon me when remembering in my mind of being around Uncle Henry from Missouri. He was such a loving person. And years later, I realized why he was such a loving person toward everyone. The secret was that he was very close to Jesus and had a personal relationship with Him. Uncle Henry also painted oil paintings of farmplaces. But all of his fences did not include gates; there was no way to get out of the fences that he painted in the paintings.

It was while we lived in that house, the big A-framed, white house, that I was very sick with tonsillitis. After suffering with the infection in my body for over a year, and after being admitted into the hospital several times, which involved being given numerous shots to fight the infection, the doctor decided to remove my tonsils. After I had the tonsils removed at the age of five, I got healthy, and I was able to gain weight.

$\maltese$

CHAPTER 5

Moving Household Event

In the winter of 1958, my family moved to the Noreen place. With us moving meant that my brother and I would be attending school district 61. This schoolhouse had a full-sized basement, where we would play basketball and the tag game in the wintertime if the weather was too cold. There were more students who attended this school, and I had two other classmates in my grade level. I was in the third grade, and Jake was in first grade. The transition was a very difficult one. The teacher's name was Mrs. Carolyn. She was young and always brought her big thermos full of coffee that she drank with her noon meal and at recess times. I used to sit beside her on the merry-go-round, and I could smell the rich aroma of the coffee that she sat sipping. The steam from the coffee inside the cup could be seen clearly on a cold day in the fall. She had long, dark-brown, shoulder-length hair that she curled under at the ends. She had short bangs that were curled toward her forehead. She wore dark-brown horn-rimmed glasses and bright, red-colored lipstick on her lips. She was very physically fit and wore dark skirts and light-colored blouses. I had the opportunity to visit her home at one time and met Mrs. Carolyn's horse named Butterscotch. He was a buckskin horse and was very well trained. She and her husband didn't have any children. I felt sad for them because I just knew that they would make wonderful parents if they had a child or children. The children at school seemed to have respect for her. She was a very quiet person, but there were times when she did get angry. When she got angry, her face would turn a bright pink, almost red in color. She would talk in very short sentences to make her point in these times. But these times were very rare occurrences.

After several years, a new teacher, Mrs. Blanche, came to the school to teach the students. She was an older woman and had grown children of her own. Her husband was a barber in the town of Albion, where they lived. This school had a school board that was made up of three or four sets of parents who had students attending the school. The prominent school board members were the Salmons, the Rygeens, and the Jacksons. If any of the students belonging to these families were mischievous at school during those hours, there wasn't a thing the other students or their parents could do about it. The school board did not have an outside party that was involved directly with the school. And believe me, all these families had at least one of their children acting up during school hours. The teacher was afraid of losing her job if she reported the incidents, so absolutely nothing was done about those incidents that were taking place during school hours. Those students who were being persecuted were forced to endure the hardships, and when they could, they would annihilate themselves from those students who were being the culprits/bullies. On top of these incidents going on, the basics of mathematics were being changed in the schools at that time. I was having a difficult time learning the new math. After the teacher assigned me to be tutored by an upper classmate who had the new math conquered, I did well in mathematics afterward.

Somehow, with the grace of God, Jake and I got through the years of being students at this country rural school but not without incident after incident happening. Life for Jake was not easy at this school either. The older boys would be at odds with him day in and day out. Then one time, Jake went home and was very fed up with these older boys. He told his older sister's husband of what they were doing to him. I guess they were even hitting Jake with a baseball bat, and everything had gone haywire with this situation. Our oldest sister's husband told Jake to surprise these boys and hit them with a baseball bat when they were mean and ornery toward him. So he did, and right away, the school board wanted to get Jake expelled from the school. But he reported that those older boys treated him differently after that incident happened. This happened at the time when I was in high school.

Outside the hours being at school, I had many enjoyable hours with my friend Lydia. And I started to enjoy my time of being alone without having to have other people around me to be happy. Although all this turmoil was taking place, Jake had Denny Gustas as a friend. I also befriended Bernadine during this time. Both of these kids had parents who were very similar to our parents. They had spiritual beliefs in God and, most of all, held principles, morals, and values high in their lifestyle. Jake and I got two bottle-fed lambs from Denny's dad. Dad bought one lamb for each of us to feed and take care of until they were grown sheep. That started us raising sheep, which was a new adventure for all of us. We fed the lambs with used soda bottles with a formula mixed up for the lambs and a special nipple at the opening of the soda bottle. That was fun at first, but then it became a chore, along with the chicken chores and pig chores that I had to do. We didn't just do our outside chores when it was summertime but also in the wintertime with ice, snow, and mud on the ground.

It was while we went to District 61 that we had field days at District 57. There I met some wonderful children to become friends with at that time. I met the Friedrick family: Bob, Jane, Verne, and Cary, who was my age. Verne and Cary ended up going to high school at the same time that I did. Our friendship led to our parents spending time with each other. I remember their house; it was very large, and it had a big basement.

During these field days, we would play games with the other children. Sometimes it was softball, soccer ball, or other inside games, which included word games, finding the "I spy" object inside the schoolhouse. At the end of the school day, we were fed treats, which included Kool-Aide. Our parents would come and get us from that schoolhouse at the end of the school day.

Despite what the world dealt me at that time, I always had my friend Lydia. She and I would walk in the evenings and sing in the long lane to the fields that my dad farmed. We lived on the Noreen place at that time and until I graduated from high school and got married in August of 1969. Some of the popular songs were country and western and these songs that were made popular by Hank Williams Sr.; Patsy Cline; Ferlin Husky; Peter, Paul and Mary; and other musical artists brought solace to Lydia and me as we sang them. We also liked to sing in Lydia's upstairs bathroom at her home. The room had an echo sound to it, and it was so awesome to sing in that room! To me it sounded like we were in a recording studio and on microphones.

Lydia always owned at least two horses, if not four. We would ride horses in the summertime, when the weather was warm. Since she had only one saddle, I usually had to ride bareback, without a saddle. The only thing I had to hang onto to stay aboard the back of the horse was a tuft of the horse's mane that wasn't shaved off, and I balanced with the calves of my legs that clung tightly to the sides of the horse. If the horse trotted, it was hard to stay on. But if I would get the horse to walk or gallop, it wasn't such a rough ride. Finally, Lydia's dad bought another saddle, and then I had to learn to ride all over again. Sometimes I would lose my balance and start sliding off the saddle, and I had to learn how to correctly place my feet/shoes in the stirrups of the saddle. I learned that wearing boots helps to keep your feet from slipping through the stirrups when riding. I remember bailing off the horse many times when I lost my balance. I would select a ditch that was clear of wild rose bushes and such gnarly brambles so that I wouldn't get all scratched up from the thorns of them. Grass provided a soft cushion to fall into at those times. The horses did have a tendency to want to gallop all the way home. Sometimes we would let them, and other times we would rein them in and insist that they walk on the path homeward bound.

One time, Lydia decided that she and I would ride double on her buckskin horse named Mocco. I got up onto the horse behind the saddle, and then she would mount into the saddle, and I would swing her leg over the saddle in front of me. This time, I no sooner got her leg swung over, and Mocco bucked us both off. She landed on top of me, and I felt pain but not like the pain later in the next weeks. As time went by, my mouth had a twitch in it, and my neck felt weird. My mom didn't take me to the doctor because no one in her life had ever broken a bone before. She did not possess the knowledge of the symptoms of a broken bone. As more time went by, the twitch in my mouth stopped. Life went by, and then later in life, I reaped the repercussions from my fall from the horse.

I always had a yearning for God in my life and enjoyed going to church every Sunday. Mom took us to church at the ALC Lutheran Church in Newman Grove every Sunday that the weather permitted us to attend. My dad only attended church on Easter Sunday and Christmas Sunday and the New Year's Eve candlelight service if we were lucky. He wasn't much for attending church. He made up a lot of excuses why he could and would not attend church services.

I helped teach vacation Bible school when I got in the seventh or eighth grade and found that I really enjoyed teaching children. Later in my life, I would expand on this gift that the Lord placed in my life.

As I entered into the high school years that I spent at Newman Grove High School, life became simpler and easier. I left all the past incidents that happened in elementary school behind me and made new friends. In fact, I made four new friends: Mary, Karey, Pearlie, and Reena. I had my eye on some of the boys, but they were either football players or upperclassmen. And most of them already had girlfriends, so they were out of my league.

So I befriended guys who Lydia knew from Lindsay and Humphey and her boy cousins from St. Berer or Corlee. But I heeded my mother's words about not getting too close to those boys and determined to just have fun and enjoy them at arm's length, so to speak. Teenage years are very complex, no matter what era a person lives in, I think. In some instances, a teenager knows how to handle the situation, and in other situations, he/she does not, like the day surrounding the incident of our president being assassinated.

I remember the day when President John F. Kennedy was assassinated. I think I was sitting on the school bus, waiting for the other kids to get loaded on it so we could go home for the day. But history states that the incident happened on November 22, 1963 in Dallas,

Texas. Maybe I was at the high school for orientation of some sort that I remember sitting on the school bus. I was saddened that someone would shoot our president and was very perplexed of what everything meant in the details surrounding the situation. I listened to what my parents talked about the situation and left such things to the grown-ups to figure out.

I had my hands full with my education taking place in my life. Going to physical education class was a challenge in the winter months. We did not wear slacks to school in those days. I would wear a skirt and top with long knitted stockings held up by the garters on my long-legged girdle. After PE class was over, I would be sweaty, so I would take wet paper towels and wash off parts of my body. I would then put my heavy clothes on again since we had to walk from the gymnasium to the high school building in the cold winter months. We were just getting started with playing volleyball and basketball in PE since we were girls. Almost every time we had to run, it would be up and down the stairs that led to the bleachers in the gym. I would fall going up the stairs and get bone bruises on the front part of my legs. It took several weeks for the bruises to heal and not show on my legs.

In high school, I did well in all of the classes that evolved around business. I think it was because those classes really interested me at that time. I also enjoyed world history class and the English classes. I had several teachers that proved interesting and unique. Miss Boutique came from a state on the eastern coast and taught American literature. And Mr. Boga was a dark-skinned, young gentleman, spoke with an accent, and was from an island somewhere. He taught the basic art class. He encouraged his students, including me, to play with the Ouija board in the back room of his classroom in the basement of the high school. After a time, I got eerie of what the Ouija board was revealing about my life and would have no more of its playing with my emotions. One of the most eerie revelations was how many children that I would have in the future and the order of their gender. Looking back, that was a blessing in disguise. I had the prewarned outlook of what life would be in the future for me.

On the home front lines, things were very difficult at times. My oldest sister, Flossie, was suffering from full-blown anorexia. Her mood swings went from being civil to cantankerous, to say the least. I watched how Flossie treated my mom, and it was not desirable. Flossie could become a tyrant and an absolute bully toward her family members. In those days, my mom allowed Flossie to cook for the family, and sometimes Mom would just help cook for the family.

People with anorexia tend to not allow themselves to eat foods that have any nutrient value to them. And they like to control other people's eating, plus just control other people. Mom usually cooked the meat portion of the meals. As our family sat down at the kitchen table to eat a meal, Flossie would invariably eat pickled beets, the fat of the meat, and green beans. She would criticize me if she thought that I was taking too large of a portion of food to eat. A lot of these times, I would get up from the table and run to the bathroom and cry. When I came back to the table to finish my meal, my dad would reprimand me for running off and crying. He didn't understand Flossie and her eating disorder at all, and he did not understand why I reacted the way I did either. I had those moments of frustration to the point of wanting to take Flossie by the shoulders and shake some sense into her. Flossie was fussed over and coddled by both of our parents. They were very unknowledgeable of how to treat the eating disorder that was present in our house, and it was causing much chaos with us children.

I guess my maternal grandmother, Thiebe, got tired of hearing the same story from my mom. She arranged with Mom that I would go and stay with her during the summers. This started when I was eight years old. Years later, I found out from Victoria that Flossie would attack Victoria's forearms, to the point in which they bled. Mom would take Victoria to the doctor and have them bandaged. This was a regular occurrence between those two. Then Victoria would take her anger and frustrations out on me. I always had a mild disposition, so I would just end up crying. So the arrangement that my grandmother made with my mom worked out for me to be rescued from all the chaos.

Looking back, I can recall why I began smoking and drinking alcohol at a young age. I was trying to escape the whole reality that was before me at home. Sometimes I felt very much alone in my world and succumbed my emotions with these two drugs (nicotine and alcohol). Life was not physically easy for me at home either. My older sister Victoria and I fought. I felt like it was mostly her fault because she would irritate me beyond measure. So the alternative that I learned throughout the years was when circumstances get tough and rough just run away, cower away, or sit and cry over hurt feelings. Many years later, I learned that Victoria had been physically abused by Flossie acting out toward her. It helped me understand why she acted the way she did toward me when we were younger. I always thought that Victoria escaped all these unpleasant moments at home when she graduated from high school and left home to live and work in a larger city.

But my mom helped me out by providing an escapeway from all of the chaos of family relationships and dynamics. Hindsight showed me what a turning point this was in my life. She arranged with Grandma Hilger to have me spend summers with her. At the age of eight, I started the ritual of spending the summers at her house. It was a very tranquil place to live—no hassles, no one condemning me, no one making me cry and making me feeling like I wasn't worth anything.

Grandma Hilger was a very quiet person, who said very little, but she formed a bond with me and eventually taught me how to cook. I enjoyed the times of washing the dishes, reading books, and watching the *Lawrence Welk Show* on the television every Saturday night. And every night at bedtime, she would take her long, gray-colored hair out of its shape of a bun at the backside of her head and brush her hair. When she was all done brushing it, she would braid it into a long braid at the nape of her neck. After she was through with this ritual, she would tell me, "Good night, my child," and pull the covers up over us for the night. My uncle Arnold lived with my grandma, and he was a man of few words also. When these two people spoke to each other, the conversation was wholesome and heard by each other. Those were very good summers to/for me.

When I stayed there, Grandma made me a rag doll was made of the yellow material from a flour sack in those days. The face of Lazy Mary was carefully embroidered onto the material, making the impression that she was sleeping with eyelids closed, and dark, reddish-colored yarn made up her hair. She only had one change of clothes, and she could sit up since the top portion of her upper legs were made out of cloth and would bend at the hip area. She was the doll that I took to bed at night.

Grandma had a tire swing that my uncle Arnold made, and it hung from one of the trees that were located close to the house. I spent a lot of time out under that tree swinging in that tire swing since my two cousins lived about six miles away from Grandma's house.

Then in the third year that I was spending the summer with Grandmother Hilger, a change took place. At that time, I didn't understand why I was now going to spend the summer with my godmother, Aunt Parlie, and her husband, Harry, and two children, Chancey and Judy. The shift was made without any forewarning or inclusion of my decision in the plans. Later in life, I learned from my sister Victoria that she and Flossie had requested that they be allowed to stay at Grandma's house during the summer. So they took turns with their stays, lasting about a week long. While they were at Grandma's house, we were not allowed to see each other. Grandma Hilger must have been strict with the rules she had put into place about our stays.

Aunt Parlie's house was a big, white, square house, similar to what Grandma Hilger's house looked like, only this one was bigger in size. While I stayed with Aunt Parlie, I would ask her every washday if I could help her with hanging clothes on the clothesline on the south side of their house. Aunt Parlie would always say the same thing, "No, you just go play and be a kid."

I learned how to ride a bike with one of the several bikes that were available. I would practice riding down the long driveway that led to their house. The driveway was graveled with stones that made it difficult to ride a bike on. So I practiced a lot with riding my bicycle up and down it. One time, I lost my balance and ran the bike down into the deep ditch with long, green grass in it on the side of the lane. I cut the inside of my hand open on the barbed wire that was on the other side of the ditch. I pushed the heavy bike back up to the house and showed my aunt Parlie what had happened. She took me over to Grandma's house, and she put some medicine on it and bandaged the cut up for me.

I learned how to play an accordion while I spent summers at Aunt Parlie's. Chancey had been taking accordion lessons and had grown tired of playing the instrument. I now own two accordions of my own. One is a big 120 bass, and the other is a 12-bass accordion. Aunt Parlie also had an upright piano similar to the one that I had at home. But our piano was brown, and Aunt Parlie's had been painted an off-white color. As the days went by, I interchanged between the two instruments, which one to practice music on for that time. I enjoyed these times immensely. Although Aunt Parlie was not like my mom, Aunt Parlie didn't sing along to any of the songs. Even though this event was not that exciting, there were other events that took place at Aunt Parlie's house that were breathtaking.

One night everyone was sleeping, except Chancey's dad, Uncle Harry. The next morning, Uncle Harry told everybody that he heard footsteps upstairs, so he decided to check it out. He caught Chancey opening up the window screen in his bedroom, and he was about to jump out of an upstairs window that night. He was sleepwalking, and he had done this action before, several times before this time. So Uncle Harry knew what to listen for late at night when he heard the boards upstairs creaking.

Another event that was fun was when I played dress up with my cousins in the upstairs of their house. Aunt Parlie had saved some of her old dresses and high-heeled shoes for the girl cousins and Judy to play with at times. Chancey never did join in the fun, so he always pretended to be someone's husband instead.

I remember vividly the time when Uncle Harry teased me about spanking me on my birthday. He carried on and on about it for a whole two weeks before it was the day of my birthday. The morning of my birthday, I woke up and went down to eat breakfast, and all I could do was sit at the kitchen table and cry. Big crocodile tears ran down my face. Aunt Parlie was silent because she somehow knew why I was all forlorn. Finally, Uncle Harry came in and sat down at the table and asked me, "Why are you crying?"

I told him between my sobs and tears, "I'm crying because you keep telling me that you are going to give me a birthday spanking."

He responded with, "I was only teasing about it. I wasn't really going to spank you." Then I asked him for a hug. I not only got a hug but a kiss on the cheek from him. In my mind, that was the best birthday present ever. You see, he was my favorite uncle.

The summers at Aunt Parlie's lasted seven years. I started staying at my grandma's when I was eight years old. And when I was fifteen, going on sixteen, I went to spend part of the summer with my sister Victoria. Victoria had been married since I was thirteen years old and lived approximately an hour away from our home. I enjoyed my time with my older sister then. Victoria made homemade cinnamon rolls and homemade pizza while I stayed with her. Victoria's husband worked long hours as an electrician and came home in the early evenings. He seemed to be very tired when he got home. He would clean up from the day's work by taking a shower, eating supper, and spending time relaxing in front of the television for the night.

Then one day, Victoria got a phone call. It was our mom, Emma, telling us that Flossie had passed away early that morning. Mom had gone into Flossie's room to see how she was doing because it was later than the usual time that she got up in the mornings. They had called the ambulance to come and take her to the hospital, but she had passed away before they arrived at the hospital. This was terrible news to hear. I was extremely disappointed that my visit with Victoria was interrupted and that I would have to return home. This too would be an important turning point in my life.

All the memories of the vicious words that had been said between Flossie and me replayed in my head. She used to say to me, "You eat so much like a pig!" And I would retaliate with, "I do not!" Her response would be, "You fill your plate full every time you eat!" I would retaliate again with, "Well, it is better than eating vinegar and fat off of the meat, like you do." All the responses that Flossie had forced on me and the different people in her life replayed in my mind. I wondered if Flossie would or could have forgiven me for all those negative things that took place in our lives. I experienced an emotional breakdown. I became violently ill with diarrhea and continuously cried. I remember very little about Flossie's funeral. My mom took me to the doctor, and he prescribed a medication for depression for me to take. The pills made me very sleepy, and I slept all day, woke up for supper, and went back to sleep for the night. I remember that it rained, and the neighbor's haystack caught on fire by the lightening. This sleeping routine went on for ten days. Finally, I was allowed to not take the pills anymore. When I woke up, I didn't have many thoughts at all about Flossie anymore.

Life was about to change for me since Flossie was no longer on this earth. Little did I know that I would be appointed to cook, help with laundering the clothes every week to help Mom, not only plant but maintain the huge garden that was grown every year. I was also assigned to have outside chores to do every day and also learn how to drive the old 1939 Ford pick-up to take lunch out to the field every day of the summer months to my dad and mom. Wow! This was a huge change from staying with Aunt Parlie and being told to go play like a kid. Some of the chores, I enjoyed doing, but washing clothes was an extensive, tedious chore since the clothes were soaked in pails in the bathtub, scrubbed to remove the stains that were in them, and washed in a wringer styled washer, with two rinse tubs to fill with water from the bathtub. If the weather was nice in the summer, I was required to hang all of the clothes on the clothesline on the north side of the house. The lines stretched out for at least ninety yards in a single strand, just north of our house. When they were brought into the house after drying, the clothes that were to be ironed were sprinkled with a water bottle, rolled up, and placed in a huge plastic bag. The unironed clothes in the bag were placed in the deep freeze to help hold the moisture in them. Standing on my feet for hours at a time, ironing all of Dad's blue-colored chambray shirts, hankies of Mom's, and all the other items containing cotton fabric were placed in the bag for ironing. Ironing the clothes was also a very tedious chore and required many hours of physical labor. All the steps of the procedure of getting the clothes to the point of ironing were a very tedious task in itself.

As a teenager, I was a lonely young woman. I tried figuring out and deciphering what things that had occurred and were occurring in my life actually meant. Living in the country brought a large amount of peacefulness, along with not knowing what actually existed in the outside world. We were not allowed to watch many television shows, much less listen to the radio. We received the *Columbus Telegram* newspaper in later years, but that was for grown-ups to read, not young people to read. I hardly knew that violence was present in other parts of the world. I didn't understand what the Vietnam era was about. I also had a minute amount of knowledge of how the troops' lives were affected by the war they were fighting for our safety.

When I entered into the world of business college in Omaha after graduating from high school, it was evident of how naive I was on things concerning the outside world (the world outside of my own, personal world). I was always for the underdog in elementary and high school days. But when I got into college, I became more aware of those people with whom I should avoid.

> Do not grow weary in doing good things
> to others, to show an example to them how
> you are to live a life holy and pleasing to God.
> (2 Thessalonians 3:13)

It seemed like girls in the newer dormitory had more issues with drugs and alcohol. I met a couple of them, and they tried to lead me down the wrong path in life. I quickly severed myself from them and their activities that were politically wrong. Those morals and values had been engrained by my mom into my life.

The roommates in my dormitory (the older dorm that contained three floors) were more mature and settled. They were all from the country and had a set agenda, which included morals and values. The one in particular with whom I had built a friendship with was Donna from North Dakota. She and I both had to work besides go to college. So we kept each other company on the weekends when

I didn't leave Omaha and remained at the dorm. Donna worked at a pharmacy that had a soda fountain bar, and I worked at King's Food Host that was popular in the bigger cities in the 1960s. I was a waitress and got quite good at it when I could remember the regular customer's orders. I remember that they had a tuna sandwich on their menu that I always ordered before my shift was done for the day. It was a tuna sandwich dipped into some breading that was deep-fat fried. I always ordered dill pickles to go with the order. They served it on a small, thick paper plate and placed a piece of aluminum foil on top of it. Since I ate it right away, I didn't have them place it inside of a white paper bag. I enjoyed my job until one day, I slipped on some ice that had halfway melted in front of the ice machine. I guess I had just sprained my ankle, so I wrapped it and kept on working. I needed that money by that time. I used my money to buy food to eat and the other small necessities that I didn't want to explain to my parents—you know, like music records, jewelry, make-up, and so on. Oh yea, I smoked two packs of cigarettes a day. I thought that I was being cool by smoking cigs.

So I went to a business college for nine months to study to become a legal secretary while dating my future husband, Richie. After I didn't make the grades with business law, I worked toward being a Dictaphone stenographer. The shorthand that I learned in high school class was not the same kind of shorthand that the college taught, so I would have to learn shorthand all over again to compare all of the abbreviations that were applied to the college's method of shorthand.

I really longed to be a beautician and work with people's hairstyles. I went to the beauty school in Omaha and got the latest fashionable haircut for myself. My hair was short on one side of my head and longer on the other side of my head. I had lost more weight because of all the walking I did in Omaha. Omaha is very hilly where I lived and where the college was, sandwiched between Dodge and Farnam streets. The grocery store and other stores were at least eight blocks away from my dormitory. Only when my roommate and friend Donna was with me to share the taxi cab fare did I take a taxi back to the dormitory with the purchases we had made for that trip. Donna was from somewhere in North Dakota. She and I spent many weekends together in the dormitory. She and I didn't have cars to drive either while we were in college. Two other roommates of ours did have cars. We shared the two bedrooms, one kitchen dorm, and a large living room, where the television was at with four other roommates. Otherwise, I walked to and from the store in the uphill and downhill terrain. I didn't complete or finish the business degree but decided to get married. I became the loving wife and soon-to-be mother I always dreamed I would become.

CHAPTER 6

Life with First Husband—My First Love

When Richie and I were in our courting years, we had a lot of fun times alone but mostly with his sisters Mary, Dary, and Katie. He owned a '61 Ford Galaxy convertible, white on the bottom and black on top. We would put the top down and drive the winding roads up to Fort Randall Dam from his parents' farmplace. Sometimes we would drive around and then stop at the old mission church that stood standing in its dilapidated state and talk about how old that church was at that time. Sometimes the whole family would meet at the place by Fort Randall Dam, where swimming was allowed, and have a picnic lunch. Those years were pretty carefree, I must say. Richie and I would go on dates to the drive-in movies in Columbus, Nebraska, or up at Lake Andes, South Dakota. If we were up at his parents' house, we would go roller-skating at the rink in Lake Andes. But I wasn't able to roller-skate; I fell down a lot and finally got discouraged enough to quit trying. Falling down was not a fun experience at all.

We had a lot of birthday parties/keg parties at his sister Sherry's house. They always included alcohol, and I didn't handle alcohol very well. I always threw up after drinking so much beer, and then I tried beer and tomato sauce, which didn't go well with me either. I finally went to drinking hard liquor, like slow screwdrivers. When Richie and I got married, the drinking for me stopped, and Richie lessened his intake also. It was a scene for the people who weren't married yet or who had been married for a while and only drank a little all night long. I was grateful when the whole cycle stopped.

After marrying Richie, I again experienced the tradition of celebrating holidays, only this time with my in-laws. We lived in Columbus, where Richie had worked in a factory that manufactured automobile seats. I worked as an inspector in a factory that manufactured glass syringes for a medical supplier.

I got pregnant just three months after getting married. Experiencing morning sickness that was severe, I was forced to quit my job. We lived an hour away from the in-laws. And after I became pregnant with our first baby, it was not a pleasant trip for me to experience because then I had motion sickness when I rode in a car. So we skipped celebrating the holiday of July Fourth with the in-laws that year since I was due to have the baby in August. Colin, a boy, our first baby, was born in the last part of August, and I became a stay-at-home mom. I thought that my mother-in-law and one of the older sisters-in-law were going to completely unravel their wits because we weren't going to join them that year for the Fourth of July. But they went on living afterward, just like I thought that they would be able to do. Hmm!

The first house that we lived in was a two-story house that had been made into three apartments on Seventh Street in Columbus. We had neighbors upstairs and down in the basement part of the house. We got acquainted with the older couple who lived upstairs. I detected that there was something weird about the man of the couple, so we moved out into a trailer house in a trailer court just, south of the viaduct. We lived there in the trailer house when Colin was born. My mom came to help me after Colin was born. She drove in a rainstorm to Columbus, and after she came, it continued to rain for at least two more days. In those days, the baby bottles were filled with the formula for the baby and then placed in a deep cooker to boil the formula inside the bottles. My mom helped with all of that procedure so that I could relax and have time with baby Colin.

After approximately a year's time, we moved to a different house on South Thirteenth Street into the main floor of that house. There was a tenant who lived upstairs who we never knew. Without me working, the finances for us were very tight. The main foods that we ate and could afford in those days were hot dogs and pork and beans. That was our mainstay meal back then. I planted a garden in the back of our house where we lived at that time.

It was while we lived in that house that I woke up one morning and couldn't move my neck. I went to the doctor, and he sent me to a specialist, who prescribed that I have therapy on my neck. I had traction therapy on my neck for two to three months. The specialist told me that I had a pinched nerve. I don't remember him taking any X-rays of my neck. If he had, he would have discovered that I had a broken collar bone on the left side from years gone by. But that was to be discovered at a later date. When he asked me what I thought this was from, I remembered that fall from getting bucked off of Lydia's horse that day when I was about twelve years of age.

I was just starting to plant the garden, so I asked the specialist if I could continue to plant the garden. He told me to get a bath towel wet with real hot water, wring out the towel, and wrap it around my neck. Then I could plant the garden, so that's how I did it. I don't remember what I planted in that garden or if we stayed there long enough to pick the produce of all my hard work or not.

Finances were lean, and Richie's uncle invited us out to Colorado, where Richie would work at the same place as Uncle Harley for the union in construction work for the state of Colorado. Richie and I left Colin with Aunt Parlie and went on a mini honeymoon, which included looking for a job and a place to live in Colorado. When we got back from the trip, Aunt Parlie was livid with me for moving our children away from her when I had allowed her to get attached to Colin. But Richie had signed up at the union for a job position, and we were moving out to Colorado to make a better living for our family. All the few personal belongings that we had at that time could fit into a small-sized U-Haul trailer. We traded in our old, white-and-black-colored 1961 Ford Fairlane convertible for a burgundy-and-black-colored 1965 Ford hardtop. We had the Kaiser Jeep, with no top on it, and the 1965 Ford hardtop when we moved out to Colorado.

Aunt Katie and Uncle Harley also found a little cabin bungalow, which was located at the base of a mountain for us to live. The landlady's house was located approximately eighteen yards from our front door. She was nice enough to us and enjoyed seeing Colin scooting around. He didn't walk until he was thirteen or fourteen months old. He had no competition and no older children to be a role model for him. He didn't see his cousins for a while at first. After about six months, we found a house in the town of Idaho Springs and lived there until we moved back to Nebraska. We lived there two years until the construction project was done. The project was building the Eisenhower Tunnel, one of the longest tunnels in the state of Colorado. The crew experienced many difficulties with mining underground waterways and springs. The tunnel also has electrical lighting throughout its entire length and white glistening tile. It was heavy work with long hours. But the outcome of all their hard work was worth it. The Eisenhower Tunnel is the longest and most beautiful tunnels that man has ever constructed. It is lit up by dozens of lights and has a slight curve to its structure. It was built under Loveland Pass.

I had just begun to sell Tupperware when I found out that I was pregnant. Once again, I found myself incapacitated to bed, with morning sickness from being pregnant. I had to give up selling Tupperware and concentrate on the pregnancy. I had two good neighbors out in Idaho Springs, Helena and Donny, who lived behind our house, had six children of their own, and Ruby and Johnny, who lived across the street, had five children of their own. Helena invited me over all of the time just to get me out of bed and out of the house. Colin played with her youngest son, David. When I was seven or eight months pregnant, Richie's aunt and uncle would load up everyone in their Chevy Blazer, along with a big bowl of homemade potato salad, a roaster full of fried chicken, a bowl of baked beans, and a couple of batches of homemade chocolate chip cookies. We would go over a different trail every weekend. His aunt and uncle had three little boys and a girl, so then Colin had someone to play with when we were with them. Aunt Katie would babysit Colin when I had my scheduled doctor's appointments. We also had dinners together on the weekend. But they had their own friends who they had known for many years out in Idaho Springs, and they spent time with them also.

One thing that I remember so well about Colorado was that Richie did not care for the landscape with the mountains. He liked the flat land, where he could see for miles what land was out there to see. Richie worked the swing shift at his job.

Two weeks before Rachael was born, my parents, sister Victoria, and my brother-in-law came out to Colorado to visit us. They were hoping that Rachael would be born while they were staying in Colorado, but she had her own plans. In fact, he was working the swing shift the night that I went into the hospital in Denver, Colorado, to experience the birth of Rachael. A friend of mine took me to the hospital in her jeep. It was snowing that night. She drove me to the hospital. Colin stayed with Aunt Katie that night. Our little girl, Rachael, was born the next day, in January, around noontime. After our baby was born, Ruby came over and helped walk the floors with Rachael since she had developed bronchitis at the age of ten days old. The doctor said that bronchitis was very common in babies about that time of the year and that he was thankful that she did not have to be hospitalized. We were very grateful too that God had given us that blessing. After the bout with bronchitis, Rachael grew and was a very happy baby.

In March, when the construction project was done, we packed up the biggest U-Haul truck and moved to back to Nebraska. Colin was two years and seven months old, and Rachael was two months old when we moved back to Nebraska. We moved to the same town where my sister Victoria and her husband lived and Richie's sister, Macy, and her husband, Lonnie, lived. Richie worked in construction in the spring's rainy season during the day. It was a hard, tedious work, and he came home exhausted. And I worked in a factory in the evenings. The children stayed at a babysitter's until Richie got home from work. We ended up having our landlady's daughter babysit the children because they lived next door to us on Square Turn Boulevard in Norfolk. She was around seventeen or eighteen years old and really took good care of Colin and Rachael. The children liked her too.

Colin especially liked the food she fed him for supper. Macaroni and cheese and hot dogs were his favorite food at that time. I worked at a factory, the night shift, where they made glass syringes—as an inspector again.

In the summer of that year, we moved to Richie's uncle Gordie and aunt Shelly's acreage. His aunt and uncle moved in a large mobile home, onto the backside of the acreage, where their family of six dwelled. Richie took a job at a cattle feeder lot. He loved being out on the tractor and doing the chores that he was assigned. His boss treated his workers well. They got a side of beef each year, and they had parties for all of the hired hands and their families. We especially enjoyed eating the many salads and mountain oysters that were pre-pared for the occasions. What are mountain oysters, you say? They are the resource that comes from farmers castrating their beef cows that become steers afterward. They are breaded and deep-fat fried— very delicious, once you get the taste of them. Eventually, Richie's aunt Shelly and uncle Gordie wanted to move into their house that we had been living in, on the acreage.

So we decided to move to Omaha. The decision to move there was a big mistake. We stayed with my uncle Kyle and aunt Judy until Richie secured a job, and we found a house. Richie was able to obtain a job after two or three months. He was only employed three weeks, and he was laid off. We had found a very small house with two small bedrooms and a basement to live. After Richie lost his job at Fruehauf's Manufacturing Company, we had to collect commodities from a food bank in order to be able to eat. I felt very humiliated from the experience of having to ask for a handout from the food pantry center.

I secured a job at a wood mill. The factory produced the wooden portion of what trophies were made out of. It was a job fit for a man to be doing. I ran a huge planer that sanded down boards of different sizes. Most of the time, at work, I would have to literally pull the boards out of the planer. I would then stack the boards onto a mov-able pallet. I wore men's leather gloves to keep my hands from the splinters of the boards. It was a hot, dry environment, and cold sores developed on my lips. There were no bottles of water available for me to have at my side on the workstation. I would have to run back and forth to the community water fountain. And each time I would have to leave my workstation, I would have to let the old grouchy man who was putting the boards into the planer on the other side know that I was leaving. I finally let my supervisor know that I and the grouchy old man did not get along, and he put me on a table saw, sawing the knot holes out of boards. At least I was working by myself and could come and go to the bathroom or get a drink as I pleased. I would get up at five o'clock in the morning and would get home at two o'clock in the afternoon. I was absolutely exhausted when I came home from work that I would eat something and then fall asleep on the sofa in the living room. After the loss of our long-distance phone service, I would call Mom via collect calls and cry because the life we were living was much too hard to bear for all of us.

Finally, Mom called me and gave us the good news that a factory, fifteen miles away from their home, was hiring welders and that Richie should come quickly to apply for a job position. I talked to Richie's sister Macy about taking care of the children because I had to stay working until we knew for sure if Richie was hired. Richie's sister Macy said that she would be glad to help out by taking care of the children. Her own children were almost the same age of our children. Richie took off in his Kaiser Jeep that had a top on it now, with the children, covers, clothes, and food for Macy's house.

He called me with good news that he was hired and had a big U-Haul truck with him, and Macy's husband, Lonnie, readied to pack everything up and move to Abion. My mom and dad had rented a house for us to move into right away. It was January in 1974. There was snow on the ground when we moved those 240 miles, now close to my parents. The house had three bedrooms and was a bungalow-style house. It belonged to my great-aunt Mabell and uncle Walt. They lived down the street from us, about two blocks. When we moved there, Colin was too young for school yet. He attended Mrs. Sharp's preschool when he was five yehars old the next year. When I took him to kindergarten roundup, he wouldn't leave my side, and he cried. So we decided that he was not ready for kindergarten. He loved it at Mrs. Sharps' preschool; he developed friends from there.

The house was very cold, and I put heavy draperies on the windows in the wintertime. In the summertime, we kept cool with fans. We spent a lot of time with my cousin Marty and her husband, Jacob, and two children, Sandy and Don. We eventually started going to the same Lutheran Church as they did. We all went swimming in the afternoons after church services were over for the day. Pastor Reinhart was related to us on the Hilgers' side of the family, but I don't remember how that came into play. I believe he was a distant cousin on Grandma Hilger's side of the family. We would celebrate birthdays and anniversaries together also. At other times, we would go out for supper (the evening meal) and then go bowling. Although the younger children, Don and Sandy, were little, they still could roll the bowling balls down the alley. It was a great fun for all of us. If we went to our house after swimming, I would fry up zucchini and hamburgers. Fried zucchini was a new commodity in those days. I didn't hear of it much; it wasn't a popular food item in those days.

Colin was getting to the age of being able to throw the softball, so Richie would spend time in the evenings doing that with him. When Richie was a young teenager, he was approached by the pro baseball leagues to go play pro baseball. It cost some money up front to join up with them, and his parents couldn't afford it then with a household full of eleven kids to raise, so he had to pass up the opportunity to play pro baseball. But he did play on Humphreys town team. He always played short stop and pitcher for their team. We always thought Colin had quite the pitcher's arm on him, like his dad had an arm on him too. He threw a rock toward the neighbor's house one time and broke a window in the neighbor's shop, which was located behind their house. I took him over there to apologize to the neighbor for breaking his window. The neighbor was elated that Colin came over to apologize and reassured him that everything was all right with him.

At another time, Colin threw a dirt clod while he and I were out in the garden, and the dirt clod hit me right square in the middle of my back. I made a fuss about it by telling Colin that the dirt clod really hurt me. We didn't spank our two oldest children mainly because they had sensitive spirits, and they usually got the jest of what we were telling them by just talking to them, like in the fact that Colin didn't ever throw dirt clods while we were in the garden after that day. He surely loved to play around in the garden while Richie and I hoed the weeds out of it. We had a big enough garden to where I could process foods for the wintertime, and we kept those jars of canned foods in our small dugout basement. We had a small basement that was located at the back of the house, where we stored our produce from the garden. We even planted potatoes and were able to preserve them in the basement, along with the jars of vegetables that I had canned to eat in the wintertime months.

Colin and Rachael were always getting into trouble together. Sometimes I wondered who was the older of the two children. Rachael acted like she was the older sister to Colin a lot of times in those years. When we were traveling in our Ford Bronco, if Colin fell asleep, Rachael would put his head on her shoulder or lap to support his neck.

We lived next door to a man and his wife who owned a blacksmith shop. It was located next door to the west of our home. The man, Bob, always rolled his own cigarettes and had the cigarette paper lying around in his workshop. Colin would go over and spend time at Bob's shop and one day came home with the cigarette papers, went into the car where Richie kept one of his cigarette lighters in the cubbyhole/glove box, rolled up several of the cigarette papers. and lit them. Instantly, he had set his face on fire! Rachael came running into the house and told me that Colin got hurt! Colin came into the house with singed lips, nose, eyebrows, and hair. I rushed him to the doctor, and the doctor examined him, applied some antibiotic ointment onto the burns, and gave me some cocoa butter to put on the burns. When we got home, I did further investigation of how this incident occurred because Colin was saying that Rachael did this to him. I finally got Colin to confess what really happened, and he apologized to Rachael for accusing her of hurting him.

Shortly after that happened, Rachael stuck gravel stones from our driveway up her nose. I took her to the doctor to get the one gravel stone that was lodged in the upper part of her nose out. The more she cried about the incident, the more lodged the stone became in the bridge of her nose. This incident happened a second time. My little exploratory, imaginative children were busy finding out different aspects of life.

In the days that we lived in Abion, Richie worked in Lindsay at the irrigation factory, welding the irrigation pipes and gearings together. I learned how to knit by taking some knitting classes, and then I also learned how to crochet with yarn. I sewed the clothes with the sewing machine for the children, and I made them wear the clothes. I also took up doing ceramics at the ceramics shop in town. It was time-consuming, and it provided a getaway from the children once a week.

I started working at the Wolfe's Memorial nursing home in 1976 as a nurse's aide. I worked the night shift so Richie would be home with the children. In March 1977, I had my first gall bladder attack at work. The doctor did not let too much time lapse before she did surgery. It was a good thing because my appendix was about to rupture when they did the surgery. I went back to work in two weeks by holding a pillow across my stomach when I lifted the patients at the nursing home.

Shortly after my surgery, Richie started feeling ill. He had a hard time swallowing his food, and he had diarrhea. I knew what the signs were, from studying some medical procedures, that those are the first signs of having cancer. We went to see Dr. Knoll in Norfolk about three times. And when he did not know what to do, I asked if he would refer us to a specialist. He sent us to Lincoln Memorial Hospital in Lincoln, Nebraska. By the time we got down there, it was June already. The doctor down there examined him and was very upset with Dr. Knoll for not sending Richie down to him sooner. They prepared Richie for surgery that was going to repair the damage that had occurred in his esophagus by the cancer. He had the surgery. But when the doctor came out to the waiting room to tell me what went on in surgery, it was not good news. My sister-in-law, Marty, was with me at the time fand I stood up and started yelling at the doctor that he had the wrong patient. It surely was not Richie, who he was telling me about such dastardly news! The doctor told me that the cancer was all over in his organs, and they had no alternative but to shut the wound from surgery and give him other alternatives to fight the cancer. After the surgery, we saw another doctor, an oncologist, who suggested that Richie try chemotherapy to fight the cancer cells. Richie was in agony of *why he* was plagued with cancer. He did not want to die; he had a wife and two kids, who he loved and wanted to take care of them. He went ahead with the decision to have one round of chemotherapy, but it did not do what we thought it would do for him. Throughout the days in the ICU unit that he was placed into was an isolated eleven-by-eleven-foot cubicle. I would go to the hospital early in the mornings and help care for him. He wanted me to read the Bible to him, so I did read to him. His parents came down to see him once a month. His mom could not stay very long and see what the disease was doing to her son. I stayed with Richie's cousin, Londa, while he was in the hospital. That's also where his parents stayed when they came down to see him.

Colin and Rachael stayed with my parents while I stayed in the hospital with Richie. Rachael started preschool, and Colin started kindergarten when year that their dad was so sick with cancer. I would call them on the phone to talk to them, and then they would come to see their dad in the hospital, maybe every three weeks or so. The time seemed long for all of us. For me to watch my beloved husband suffer with cancer and all that was involved in his last days here on earth was painful.

Before Richie got really sick, we were able to go fishing together as a family up at his parents' part of the country. He wanted to go to the Lincoln Zoo, so we all went to the zoo for an afternoon. He also was released for a weekend from the hospital before he started the chemotherapy. He spent it at Londa's house, and all of his siblings and parents came down to Lincoln to see him and visit him. He had lost a lot of weight by that time and didn't look like himself. That was the last time they saw Richie alive. He died at the hospital with his parents and me with him on September 19, 1977. I'll never forget the date and time because Elvis Presley died the month before Richie on the sixteenth day of August in 1977.

We had two funerals for him: one in Albion for all of his coworkers, friends, and relatives who lived around that area and one up at Spencer, where most of his relatives and pastime friends lived. He is buried in a country cemetery that is connected with the country church, where he went to church when he was a boy and young man. I will be buried there someday when it's my turn to die.

Life for me was rough after Richie died. I didn't know Jesus as my personal Savior, which I'm sure that Richie did before he died. I didn't realize how dependent I was on Richie. We did almost everything together and spent a lot of hours, days, months, in the eight short years we were married together. I did not possess a sense of direction in my life. At one time, I remember thinking about moving to Grand Island and attending beautician schooling. I always desired to be a beautician. I guess you could say that I was very lost and felt very much alone. My parents lived close by, but I don't remember leaning on them very much for comfort in my sorrow those days. I was not provided a support team in the time of my deepest sorrow. I had made a friend with Jean, who was the mother of one of the kids that Colin went to school with in those days. But she seemed to be busy with her husband and kids. I had no one who could understand the grieving I was walking through at that moment in time.

I couldn't eat for about four to five months after Richie's death. I was taking Shaklee vitamins and lived off those for those few months. I fed my kids macaroni and cheese and a lot of hot dogs. I must have overindulged with the hot dogs because Colin told the mom of one of the neighbor kids he played with that he and Rachael ate lots and lots of hot dogs, out of the mouth of a babe! The neighbor lady sent home a huge beef steak with Colin one day when he had been over there, playing with her son. I was so embarrassed that Colin had told that lady about what food I cooked for the kids.

I didn't take the opportunity to turn to anyone for help in those days and wandered around aimlessly. I started frequenting the bars in other towns and hung around this one couple who liked to drink. I approached this one guy, Don, who was my age, but he was busy with his own life. Don was there the day that I bought myself a horse at the sale barn in Abion. When I bought the horse, I told the auctioneer that I would be getting my money back if the horse didn't work out. Sure enough, the horse had been drugged. And when I test rode the horse outside of the arena, in the April-rainy-day weather, he starting running, and I had no choice but to bail off (jump and roll on the ground) him. I wasn't ready to give up on the horse, so I led him down to a small arena, and Don and my other friend helped me get the horse saddled up. I no sooner got in the saddle that the horse reared up, threw me off, and rolled over on me. The horse stood about twelve to fourteen hands high, a big horse, so it was like I was rolled over on by an elephant or something. I got up and could barely walk. After Don helped me lead the horse back to the sale barn to get my money reimbursed, I checked myself out at the emergency room at the hospital. The doctor told me that I had torn tendons and ligaments in my lower back. He recommended that I go home and relax, take some hot baths, and rest. I went home and soaked in the bathtub and drank a few beers to relax. In about two to three weeks, the soreness was gone. It remained in my fantasy about Don, but nothing became of those dreams and ideas. Then years later, my mom shared with me that he had a violent temper. That would have been a great thing to place in my children's and my life!

I finally started visiting with Jean and her family. I would go over after school and visit to pass some time away for the day. She and I were visiting one day, and she mentioned that she knew this young guy, Trent, who liked kids and how good he was with kids. So finally, he came to visit them. He brought the kids each a box car toy. Jean's kids basically hung on him and seemed to really like him. He seemed weird in a way to me. He really wasn't my type. He was too skinny and had a mustache. But it ended up that he and I spent some of the evening out together. At the end of the evening, he asked me, "Do you believe in love at first sight?" and I answered with no. But we started seeing each other anyways.

❧

CHAPTER 7

Life with Second Husband

Trent and I started seeing each other and eventually planned to marry. But the dating period had really been short-lived, it seemed, when I stood looking back in hindsight. Then right before we were supposed to get married, his true color started to erupt from down under, but I was too codependent at the time to recognize what was going on with Trent. I thought that he would somehow get better. I ignored the red flags that were imminently visible at that time. I had never been around a person who had come from the dysfunctional family that he had been brought up with in his life. I had not learned about any of the effects that dysfunction has on the family members. Therefore, I could not and did not recognize the behaviors of someone who had family dysfunction in his life. I thought that if I could just talk some common sense to that person, he/she would just snap out of that mood or behavior. But it didn't work that way with Trent. He had practiced such behaviors to his advantage for too many years in his life. I was not knowledgeable about manipulating people and their underlying motives to win their way in life, which leads me to share with my readers the psychological aspects of my life, those that explain why I am the person I am today.

I'd like to explain the dynamics of the dysfunctional dilemma that I entered not only into my life but my children's lives as well. I was codependent, which means that I did not know what healthy and functional were for sure. I thought that I could somehow fix Trent.

What is statistically normal behavior is not necessarily healthy or functional. For instance, it was once statistically normal to beat children with sticks, boards, belts, and whips, but we now see this as child abuse, which is a dysfunctional behavior (Friel and Friel). A lot of the times, when parents are physically disciplining their children, their own anger and hostility are being portrayed outwardly toward the child being disciplined. We have found that other methods of discipline are better and work better than the old methods. Giving a child a time-out does not necessarily lower their self-esteem, in comparison to beating him/her with an object. I had not experienced or witnessed my dad and mom being violent with each other, but I myself had experienced humiliation from my dad when I cried as a reaction to my sister, Flossie, when she would verbally abuse me at the meal table almost every day of my life while I lived at home those years.

When I was lonely, in 1977, after my husband's death, I could have done some very positive things, but I did not do those things. I could have called a friend and talked for a while. I could have written in a journal for my thoughts and feelings. I could have sat quietly and embraced the loneliness for a while. I could have reached out to a group of people who had the same problem that I was having at that time. It seemed that my whole support system—my parents and my cousin Marty and her husband, Jacob—all abandoned me. I had no one to talk to in order to gain any wisdom of what to do with my life and for the benefit of my children's lives. I seemed to be dependent on people, whether they had good or bad influence on my life.

I believe that my codependency started when I was a child with the dilemma of living with my sister, Flossie, who was afflicted with anorexia and in the situation with my other sister, Victoria, who was acting out verbally toward me. She herself was being physically afflicted by our sister, Flossie, who was afflicted with anorexia. The whole problem was avoided by my mom sending me to my grandmother's house to live for the summers. It was a temporary solution for the problem that existed. But the serious problem did not go away.

Remember I mentioned that I started smoking nicotine and drinking alcohol at a very early age of fifteen or sixteen years of age? That was my coping mechanism at the time. Plus, when Flossie died,

I was given the medication to have me sleep for ten days in a row. I had not developed any coping mechanisms regarding grieving the loss of a loved one. My alcohol consumption increased after Richie died. Again, I did not have any positive solution to the problem that I had at that time. I had not learned about boundaries or that boundaries could exist in my life.

Boundaries usually overlap one another. I did not know that a person should have boundaries. There are emotional boundaries, intellectual boundaries, social boundaries, sexual boundaries, time boundaries, and money boundaries (Friel and Friel). I was not given the opportunity to recognize or address my true feelings about how my sister Flossie treated me and my family members. I wasn't given opportunity to identify the wrongs that happened to us as children at school and in the home. I was not given the opportunity to identify and vent my feelings about those wrongs; I wasn't even allowed to talk about those feelings I had at that particular time in my life. I also didn't make a decision about my relationship with Victoria in concern with hurting me with words. I did not learn to let go of the uncontrollable episodes in my life until late in my life. I had not learned the most subtle, powerful and magnificent ways to live a comfortable life. Does this sound like deep philosophy to the readers of this book? Isn't life deep at times? To me, life is almost always deep.

During the thirteen years of my second marriage, we moved around a lot. We moved approximately fourteen to fifteen times in eleven years' time period. We were always isolated from people, plus pulled away from my parents and family. Trent worked for various hog confinement companies in the states of Iowa and Nebraska. We had a baby girl, Mackenzie, two years after we were married. And whenever I was distraught about something in life, she would seem to be able to sing a song that would uplift my spirits and give me hope.

Two years later, I had my last son, Justin, in May of 1982. When I was almost due to have Justin, Trent took a job at a hog confinement by a small town in South Dakota. We moved twice from the hog confinement, where we had been living for two years to a small town in Nebraska. When I tried to put Rachael in the school system where we were moving to, they told me that she was too far behind to attend school there. Since we were going to move to South Dakota anyway, Trent borrowed his parents' tagalong camper and took Rachael with him to attend school, where she would end up anyways. After the month trial period was up, Colin and Mackenzie and I, who was pregnant with Justin, joined him at the house in South Dakota.

We lived in a split-level house that was only two years old. It was out in the country, and the older children started out going to school in a school located along one of the main highways. The children made friends quickly, but I was at home with the two younger children, ages newborn, two years and three months old. Later in life, I learned that Trent was fired from at least three jobs because he was caught stealing from his employers.

Shortly after moving there, I joined an aerobics group in a town called Cheser, and that provided a night out of the house for me. When Justin was about a half year, and Mackenzie was a year and a half old, I had found an older lady who would come to our home to babysit the children. We knew her as Grandma T. I went to work at a nursing home and met my friend Peg, who I would later in life also work with at the Evergreen Terrace Nursing Home. I worked evenings for about a year. One night, when I left work, it was snowing, and the wind was blowing. A blizzard had started to form, but that didn't stop me because I was driving Trent's four-wheel drive pick-up that night. The snow was coming down so hard that I had a very hard time seeing where the road was for sure. I found myself driving in and out of the shallow ditches. Then I turned the corner onto a different road, and I hit a patch of ice that was under the snow-packed road, and down in the ditch I went. After several attempts of backing out of the ditch, I had no choice but to walk back to Grandma T's house. I walked for about a fourth of a mile with my flashlight and knocked on their door. They woke up, and Grandma T provided the couch in the living room for me to sleep on and gave me a pillow and a blanket to cover myself with for the night. I called Trent in the morning, and he came to help pull out the pick-up with one of their tractors. Shortly after that, I quit the nursing home, but I was not content to just stay at home.

So I tried to sell Avon. I had sold Avon before where we had lived before we moved, which provided a profitable business. I took a country route first and then added a town route onto my business. I couldn't make as good of a profit from the area that I was in for some unknown reason. I believe it was because the farmers weren't as wealthy as they were where we lived before. And there were probably Avon representatives who were servicing people outside of their territories.

While we were living at that hog confinement house, Trent told me about an acreage that he thought would be good to purchase to put the horses on to graze. After he lost his job at that hog confinement, we had to rent and move to a big, square, white house by Chester, South Dakota. We decided that Trent would attend school, and I would work in Sioux Falls so that we could carpool, since we only had one car at that time. We also decided that we would build a full-sized basement and move a house in to place on top of that basement. There was this couple who had just built a new house, and they wanted to sell the house that they had been living in. The price was right, so we bought the house and moved it with a moving company, fourteen miles to the acreage we were buying. Shortly after, we moved house onto the acreage; we purchased an old school bus that had been painted dark blue with a white top. I learned to drive it and used it to haul the Missionette girls from our church to summer camp in it.

We started working on building with cement blocks the basement of our house that summer while I was working in Sioux Falls at a nursing home. I didn't take a particular section of the nursing home to work when I was at the Good Samaritan in Sioux Falls so that I would have variety in my work. I was a certified nurse's aide and knew the ins and outs of the job position. When we were done with the house, my parents came to visit us. We had then purchased an old, single, wide trailer house and parked it farther back on the property. That is where my parents slept overnight while they were visiting us. We put an electric heater in the front room of the trailer so that they would be warm while they slept overnight.

It was there that I met a young lady, who became a friend I would keep for many years. I was in charge of training her. Later, when she was looking for work, I guided her to the same nursing home, where I first had worked in Madison. Beth and her boyfriend, at the time, didn't have a place to stay, so we housed her and her boy-friend in our basement. Shortly after that, they found a cute house in Madison to rent. I have stayed in touch with Beth ever since that period of time. She has recently settled down in the western part of South Dakota.

When Trent started his business, I tried to work in Howard at a nursing home. The distance was long, and it was wintertime. After traveling treacherous roads to and from work, Mackenzie and Justin were sick almost continuously. I decided that I would have to cut back in order to stay at home. I remember making seven loaves of homemade bread every three days and fixing soups and casseroles for my family to eat to get by with what finances were coming into the house. Trent started working at the Honey Factory in a neighboring town until he built up his clientele at the shop. And looking back, I don't know if Trent was lying to me about the finances, but I seemed to be in a place at the time where I just had to trust his word.

Looking back at my life with Trent, I can totally understand the concept of women who are mentally and emotionally abused. There's a certain point in a marriage when it seems that a person feels like she's too far in to ever get out of the situation that has gone totally wrong. That's where I was at that time of my life in my marriage. It takes another person to enter that person's life and act as a support system to help them get out of the bad situation that they are in at the time.

I had an older woman, Helena Johanson, who was a devoted Christian, who came alongside me and gave me some very wise advice. She told me to save some money for my children and myself. At the right time, I would be able to financially be set to support my children and myself when Trent and I would separate. I heeded her advice and was very well prepared for that time when it eventually did come to take place.

There were a lot of lies that were said by Trent and a lot of deceptions that took place that broke down the bond of love and trust between us. I can't respect a person who continuously lies and lives a life full of deception. How can any human being completely trust someone who is supposed to cherish them and love them and shows the opposite characteristics than those of love? What I realized at a later time in life was that Trent had been fired from most of the jobs that he had worked at in the eleven years we were married. The scriptures talk about how the husband is to be submissive to God and therefore then will be able to treat his wife as Christ does the church, with much love and mercy. Ephesians 5:25–33 says that husbands are to love their wives, just as Christ also loved the church and gave Himself for it. And Trent claimed to be a born-again Christian, but he hardly ever acted like he had made any commitment of such. Ephesians 4:23–29 states that we are to be renewed in the spirit of our minds and that we are to put on the new man, which was created according to God in righteousness and true holiness. Each one of us is to speak the truth to one another so that we can be members in Christ, being kind to one another.

After the thirteen drawn-out years of marriage that I experienced with Trent, I sought counseling in many perspectives. I was wondering what was wrong with me for most of the time because I was told by not only Trent but by the first pastor who gave us counseling that I was not doing what I was supposed to be doing. Trent was never told that he was not living according to the standards that he claimed he had committed to according to the scriptures.

Finally, getting marriage counseling with a certified successful counselor was a learning experience for me. I began to recognize my rights as an individual person and gained strength in being advised to give ultimatums and boundaries regarding my life. With the support of my counselor, I was able to stand firm with the ultimatums that I gave Trent concerning his actions and deeds. Somehow, having the support from someone on the outside gave me the strength that I needed to make changes in our lives. I once was told by a woman pastor that if you don't rock the boat, changes will never occur in any situation. Well, I rocked the boat, and huge changes that were positive occurred in our lives. I was about to begin a new direction and journey that I had not ever experienced in all my life. I also would be living with the results of Trent's actions toward me and my children for the rest of my life. Some of us had been verbally and emotionally abused, and some of us had been physically violated. The children went through counseling for periods of time throughout their lives to recover from the trauma that they had experienced and survived. Everyone reacted differently to the counseling and therapy that they had been involved in at the various times in their lives. I involved myself in a codependency group a couple of years later in my life when I was single again. Not until later in my life did I make a decision about the relationships that I had during this time in my life. When I entered into the next phase of my life, I still could not distinguish what was normal and what situations I should choose as a battlefield for my own relationships with other people.

In those thirteen years of my second marriage, there were good times concerning the children and myself. We lived in the country, so each of the children had their own horse. Each also had their own Chihuahua dog to sleep and play with in the house. In the wintertime, they went on snowmobiles in the snow and sledding in the hills just north of our home. In the summertime, they went swimming in the lakes that were around our town in South Dakota. In the years of 1987 through 1988, I homeschooled all four of the children. Life was quite peaceful in those days and a more relaxed lifestyle for the children and me.

We belonged to an Assembly of God church, so we participated in vacation Bible school and in summer camps. I helped the youth pastor and his wife organize and form the Missionette and Royal Ranger programs in our church for the children. Every Wednesday night, we had the Missionette and Royal Rangers meetings in the classrooms for the children to attend. There were six of us adults who taught the classes every Wednesday night. It was a lot of fun for everyone. We all learned a lot from the lessons. Badges were given to the children who knew their Bible verses. About three years later, Rachael became the first Honor Star participant to attend the state honor ceremony. She also went on to the highest honor with the Missionette program and was given a beautiful ceremony at our new church that we attended down in Sioux Falls, South Dakota.

We lived in a two-story square-shaped house while we were building the basement for the house in the country. It was while we lived in the big, square-shaped house that Justin decided to ride his worm-shaped toy with wheels on it down the upstair steps of the house. Consequently, he broke his arm at the elbow. He looked so tiny to be wearing the cast that had to be on his arm for that duration of time.

The house in the country we bought to move onto (the acreage) was bought and moved in by the house movers that we hired. The house that we moved to our acreage was moved fourteen miles. The acreage consisted of 17.8 acres. It had a large pasture and two shelterbelts of trees and thickets. It was a big project and finally was done in the end of August 1984. We had the electric company hook it up to the main electric lines along the road. We hooked up to rural water because the well on the place had a high content of iron, which made it undesirable to drink. We built a full-sized basement made of cement blocks to set the house on top of it. That took all summer to build. The older children and I all helped with putting the cement blocks down into the hole to be cemented into place for the basement walls. Trent did all the cementing of the blocks together. The house was heated with propane gas, so we had to buy a big propane tank to set closer to the road and not the house. There was a lot of details that went into building a basement. We lived in the country with our nearest neighbor about a half mile from our place.

Justin was allergic to cow's milk, so I decided that I would acquire a couple of nanny goats and milk them for our milk supply. I started with two nanny goats, and in four years, I had acquired five nanny goats and eleven kid (young/baby) goats and a billy/male goat. The milk was wonderful for making homemade ice cream, pudding, and for cooking in general. It had a lot less fat content, so it was good for all of us to drink.

In November of 1984, I committed my life to the Lord by making a conscious decision to let Him live in my heart and to have Him as my guide through my life. Life doesn't stop when a person has a heart that aches. Hard times come our way, whether it be financial, relationships, or health issues. I began to lean on Jesus's Word to help me through all issues of life. I learned through attending a church regularly that I needed the same scriptures that Jesus gave His disciples to believe in through the difficult times in life. I have gained a lot of emotional strength throughout the years since taking the

Lord's scriptures from the Bible and believing in them, standing on all of God's promises and good things that He has in store for me and my children.

When everything that was hidden was revealed in the situations concerning our lives, distinct decisions were made concerning the children's and my welfare. We continued going to the same church even though Trent's private affairs had been dealt with by the pastor that we had and the deacons of the church. Then shortly after this incident happened, my children and I were sitting in a pew toward the back one Sunday morning, and the pastor just blatantly announced to the congregation what sinful things Trent had been doing to his family and what concerned our family in general. I got up and walked out of that church that Sunday morning with my children in tow and never went back.

Later that week, I called up one of the deacons whom I knew would be empathetic with my situation and requested a meeting with the deacons, and the pastor was to attend this meeting. So the meeting was held, and the pastor and three deacons were present. Only one of the deacons empathized with me and understood why I was so distraught about the whole situation.

I finally concluded that the children and I were better off attending another church far, far away from those people. The Lord led us down to Sioux Falls Assembly of God church. Pastor T. arranged that Trent and I get marriage counseling through the church's professional counselor. The first meeting with Pastor G., who was the counselor, was with me alone, telling him my side of the story concerning my marriage with Trent. He stated to me afterward, "You paint a picture that is quite dark in my view of what your marriage is like with Trent." Then we had two counseling sessions with the pastor, and the pastor met with me alone afterward. He advised me, "I see no reason why you shouldn't divorce Trent since he was not leading you or his family in the ways of the Lord, let alone having concern for our welfare or future." I hung in there a little longer until an incident with the law happened concerning Trent and then with the counsel of Pastor T. He said to me, "You need to give Trent an ultimatum of giving up his sinful ways or lose his marriage and family." Trent didn't take me seriously, so I was given no choice but to pursue finding a divorce attorney. I made the mistake of hiring an attorney from our town, and he was worthless for my benefit. I heard of an excellent attorney from a neighboring town, who was tough on men who had criminal backgrounds. When I called him, he advised that I contact Mr. B, who was an excellent divorce attorney. So I contracted and hired Mr. B, and it turned out that he was an upstanding Christian man besides an excellent attorney.

The Lord led situations and circumstances to where we were able to become delivered from the harassment in our lives. As soon as this took place in our lives, and I had decided that I and my children had had enough of all the abuse that was initiated toward us, I was riddled with depression and anguish.

I had been an officer in an organization called Women's Aglow International for three years and remained with our chapter of the organization until it collapsed in 1992. I had held the offices of correspondence secretary, recording secretary, and treasurer. Those other women who also were officers stood by me in my time of need. Joanna, who was the vice president of Women's Aglow International, gave me very wise counsel at that time. She advised me to surround myself with God's scriptures, and I took her counsel to heart. Within a very short time I was strong enough to make life decisions for myself and my children. Some of the scriptures that I dwelled on and believed in at that time were the following:

> I put my trust in You God, in whom shall I
> be afraid what can man do to me. (Psalm 56:11)

> For I know the thoughts that I think toward
> you, says the Lord, thoughts of peace and not of
> evil, to give you a future and a hope. Then you
> will call upon me and go and pray to me, and I
> will listen to you. And you will seek me and find
> me when you search for me with all your heart.
> I will be found by you, says the Lord, and I will
> bring you back from your captivity; I will gather

you from all the nations and from all the places
where I have driven you, says the Lord, and I will
bring you to the place from which I cause you to
be carried away captive. (Jeremiah 29:11–14)

I trust in the Lord with all my heart and lean
not to my own understanding. (Proverbs 3:5)

I did a lot of praying, and the women stood behind me with their prayers. I thanked God for being a steadfast God; for getting me through poverty and famine, through heartache and distraught, through sickness and in health, through depression and happiness/hopefulness, through fatigue and energetic times, through turmoil and peaceful/refreshing times.

God moves in mysterious ways. As soon as the two years of marriage separation began, I went to San Antonio, Texas, for a Women's Aglow International conference, and Rachael went on a mission trip through the Sioux Falls church to Guatemala. We were very blessed that year that these two events took place. Rachael came back a changed young teenager, and I came back changed also.

During the very short time, occurring in the two years of marriage separation, the Lord led me to create a singing ministry for me to be involved with to mainly help me to heal from the wounds afflicted upon my life. I met a man, who actually was my piano tuner, who played the piano beautifully. He possessed a recording studio, where he recorded the songs that I requested that he record for me to sing during my ministry sessions. I sang at a number of the Women's Aglow meetings in different areas and also in churches who had heard of my ministry. They invited me to come and minister to the people that were invited for the gatherings. I had put together flyers of the songs that I would sing and I preached and taught on the principles of God in between the songs that I sang. My dear friend Terrance took pictures of me to put on the front of the flyers. As I ministered to the hurts of the other women, God healed my wounds and hurts that I had experienced in life. I became stronger than I ever was before. It was beautiful how God orchestrated it all.

CHAPTER 8

Life In Between—with No Husband

Once I was divorced, I had to seek a job. When Trent left our home, so did Colin. He was seventeen years old and very rebellious toward me for divorcing the person he then called dad. He went and lived with a friend of his in town and got a job. Later he came to me and wanted to buy a different vehicle, so I cosigned for him to help him out with that situation. I still loved him, maybe even more than before. That first winter, I clothed him with a heavy jacket and new shoes. He stayed in town while Trent served prison time in the South Dakota State Penitentiary.

We stayed in touch with Colin, and eventually, his wounds were partially healed. To this day, he has not wrapped his brain around what really happened to our family members, nor, for that matter, what really happened to him in the whole ugly situation. He was abused by the person he still calls dad. An earthly dad is a person in your life who is appointed and placed in a child's life to provide for the child and protect the child. This dad did not provide very well and surely did not protect the children in this situation. And there is a lot of psychological manipulation that goes along with the whole situation. Colin was the only one who has not sought any psychological counseling for his younger childhood years' trauma that he experienced that I know. It seems that he has not truly turned his heart to God to help him through all of life's problems that he faces each day. It seems that he has an inner desire to turn to God, but vices in his life hold him back in that area of his life. I'm praying that someday he will break loose of those strongholds and will give his life to the Lord completely. That is my prayer as his mother. But for right now, he relies on his own intuitive and knowledge for solutions to life's problems. And his mother remains faithful in her prayers for his salvation that will bring freedom to his life here on earth and eternal life in heaven with God, Jesus, our Savior.

I was faced with having to find some kind of work to bring in some money for my little family. The divorce had not been declared yet, and no child support was set into place yet. I didn't qualify to receive food stamps since I was considered owner of real estate, which was the acreage that we owned and lived on. I met and became good friends with Jamie Miner and her three daughters through going door-to-door with the promotion of getting Trinity Bible Network on the townspeople's television cable company. Over a period of time, Jamie and I became close enough in our relationship to be considered sisters. We always told each other that we were sisters in the Lord because we had equal faith in Him. Jamie received food stamps, and she shared with us her abundance of food. In turn, we would help her keep her house clean and in orderly fashion. We would spend Saturdays cleaning her two-story apartment from top to bottom.

So we were fed through her generous outstretched arm of love, but I was seeking the Lord's direction for my own source of food for my family. One day, I was driving by the one food store in Madison, and the Lord directed me to a dumpster that was located on the east end of one of the grocery stores in our town. I stopped and went over to the dumpster to see what was there for food. And to my amazement, there on top of everything else in the dumpster was a large box filled with assorted cookies. There must have been twenty packages of cookies, none of them expired in that large box. I took it to the car and examined each package thoroughly and could not detect anything outdated or wrong with the cookies. In the meantime, before this event took place, Justin kept asking me every time we entered a grocery store for the new Oreo kind of cookies with the white frosting on the outside of them. I'd always tell him the same thing, "No, we cannot afford the price of those cookies. We need other groceries more badly than cookies right now." I hurried to Jamie's apartment where she lived and showed what I had found and shared those cookies with her. We were both so elated about my find!

Along with providing food for my kids, I had to get to work to earn some money for the bills that kept coming in the mail. In the Midwest states, it is not uncommon for farmers to desire to have their fields manually depleted of weeds, so they hire people to actually pull the weeds (row upon row) out of their soybean and cornfields. Rachael and I got a job pulling and chopping weeds out of a soybean field. I was hired as the supervisor of the ten young teenagers that helped get the soybean field free from the sunflowers, milkweeds, and other weeds that existed in the field. We got up early in the mornings, around four o'clock, and met at the field around five o'clock and started our job. The summer sunrise was barely in view. We quit at two o'clock in the afternoon when the sun became too hot to work in for the day. After we had completed that job, we worked for another farmer, doing the same procedure with his soybean and cornfields. Then a third job for another farmer was done.

After all of the fields were cleaned, and those types of jobs were done, I found a job at a restaurant, where I took the position as a short-order cook. Rachael stayed home with the children while I worked. I made up all of the salads for the salad bar and set up the salad bar in all the ice. When the main cook left for the day, I would cook the orders for customers: hamburgers, fries, and so on. I cooked all the short orders for customers for approximately four months.

I applied at a home health care facility and was hired to travel and take care of specific elderly patients, who needed help in their homes. Sometimes I would help the patient by giving them a bed bath and doing their dishes and sweeping the floors. At other homes, I would do major housecleaning. And still, in other homes, I would do laundry and dishes, vacuum floors, and dust for them. Whatever their needs were, I would do them. I will never forget the one elderly lady who I took care of in her home. She had experienced a stroke, was bedridden, and required a bed bath with a change of clothes a couple times a week. As I bathed her, I noticed bruises on her back and buttocks areas. I reported these findings to my supervisor, and the elderly lady was placed in a convalescent home. Her husband was an alcoholic and left signs of abuse with the marks on his wife's behind. These were signs of his outraged anger. He later died of alcoholism.

Later, in years to come with meeting and marrying my third husband, Will, I found out that I had taken care of his ex-wife's great-uncle and great-aunt in their home, also his ex-wife's grandmother in the nursing home, where I had last worked before moving to attend college.

It was in this time frame that I was led to share my love of God with my maternal grandma and my dad. As a result, they both prayed the sinner's prayer with me and accepted Jesus into their lives. It was about two years before both of them passed away. I have no other thoughts not to believe that they are both in heaven because of their decisions that they made at that time.

In 1979, I had studied to become a certified nursing aide while we lived in Iowa and had worked in other nursing homes, so I had prior experience in this career. After I had worked for the home health care facility for about six or seven months, I applied at one of the nursing homes in Madison, South Dakota. I was hired in 1990 and worked there until we moved to the bigger town in South Dakota in 1992, where I attended college. I really enjoyed working there. One of my old friends, Peg, worked there, and we had many, many joyous times while we worked together at that nursing care home. I became the "shower/bath queen" because the director of nurses observed how the residents at the home enjoyed their time of bathing when I worked with them. I would mostly give them whirlpool baths, which was good for their circulation and physical health in general. Some of the elderly women would be suffering from dementia, but when I would strike up a song that was from their childhood, they would join in and sing along with me. We would have a time of laughter, and that is always good for the soul. That's what I have heard anyways!

I enjoyed my position as the "shower/bath queen" until one morning, Sheila worked with me. She was the one in charge of the residents' baths when I had my days off. There was a trick to keeping yourself safe in the tub room while doing all of the baths. The trick was to always, always lay down the thick mats with holes in them around the side of the tub, where you would get the residents out of the tub! But I didn't know that Sheila did not practice this safety tip, and I must admit that we were in a hurry that morning to get one bath done before breakfast. Well, everything was going well until we raised the resident out of the tub and swung her around to the place by the tub, where we dried residents with towels and dressed them. As I was walking around the side of the tub, my one foot slipped on a patch of water, and down I went onto the bathing room floor. My right arm flew back behind my head, and my shoulder felt pain right away after this happened. Needless to say, I was hurt. Sheila was torn two ways: She knew she had basically caused the mishap by not putting down the mats, and she was sorry for me being hurt, and she was afraid she would get into trouble for not obeying the safety rules of the bathing room.

After receiving therapy on my hurt shoulder and cortisone shots, which did not resolve the situation of pain, I needed surgery to relieve the pinched nerve that was causing the pain. I was not prepared for the aftereffects of the surgery, but I somehow survived it all. I woke up from having surgery and looked in the direction of my right shoulder, where a drain bag containing blood and other fluids existed. I was in pain from the surgery, and they were pumping me full of morphine, which I found out makes me violently ill, causing me to vomit. My dear friend Mara just happened to come and visit me and asked me what they were giving me for pain. She acted as my advocate and ordered the hospital staff to stop the morphine immediately. They then gave me shots to relieve the pain I was experiencing.

My oldest daughter, Rachael, came to the hospital and took me home. She was dear enough to help me bathe and dress after each bath. They put staples in me, so changing dressings of the incision was not necessary. It wasn't long, and I was put back to work on light duty. I talked to my workers' compensation agent about my rehabilitation process and informed her about me being enrolled to start college classes in September of 1992. I was given the job of helping in the kitchen and washing all the dishes in the big commercial dishwasher. The racks of dishes were very heavy for me at that time, and

I had to work slowly and diligently. Eventually, it didn't take as long of a time to get the task done.

Rachael graduated from high school in May of 1992. We had a celebration afterward at the senior center in Madiville. Her uncle Wayne and aunt Meg, plus a lot of other people, were there for the celebration.

In August 1992, I was able to quit the job and move to the bigger town, where I would be attending Dakota Wesleyan University for classes in nursing. In July of that year, my sister-in-law, Meg, called me on the phone and asked if I would be coming soon. Actually, I was going there that week to take the entrance exam for college. She told me right on the phone that she and her daughter had decided to let me and my children live in their trailer home for the duration of time I was in college. I was elated about that decision and made arrangements to stop by and visit them that week.

Before Meg had called me, I had a dream several times of the layout of a house that had three bedrooms and one and a half baths. I did not know ahead of time what the layout of the trailer was, but when I went to see Meg and her daughter, I found out that the trailer had three bedrooms and one and a half baths. I felt so elated that God would give me an inside view of what our future held for us. I felt His love and compassion for providing us a home that would only cost us the lot rent and utilities for the two years that I intended to attend college. I went into college and signed up for the nursing training, which took two years. After my first semester, I found out that I was better at counseling than nursing, so I changed my major to human services instead of nursing training. This degree would take four years to earn instead of the two years for the nursing degree. But God is good and moved Meg's heart to let us stay living in the trailer the extra two years until I had the degree completed in May of 1996.

The trailer home was in need of some repairs, and I talked with Meg's husband, Wesley, about who would have to do the repairs and who would pay for each repair needed. The kitchen floor had several holes in one corner. The flooring under the washer and dryer area needed to be replaced. I called up the church in that bigger town where I knew we would be attending and asked if there was a man there who could fix a floor, and I was given a name of a gentleman named Mike. We made arrangements for the floors to be covered with new plywood, and he completed the job. I bought a piece of kitchen carpet and laid it down on the new kitchen floor myself. I also pulled the carpet out of the main bedroom and replaced that carpet, plus laid carpet in the long hallway of the trailer house. God gave me wisdom and had me recollect knowledge from the past to help me throughout the years that I lived life alone with my three younger children.

When we attended the Assembly of God church, Pastor B. had formed an adult singles group. Most of us had been married at one time, but there were a few who had never been married yet. Our range of ages varied. We gathered together and roast hot dogs for supper and marshmallows afterward. We met at different houses and had the evening meal together. One time, I remember we all brought our pizza ingredients and made homemade pizzas at Byran's house. We played volleyball on Sunday afternoons by the church, where Sue had friends attend. We always included the kids if we wanted to do that.

The girls and I were in the praise and worship team. Rachael would sing with Matt, one of the single guys who was old enough to be her father. He was a good, spiritual role model for her though. My other daughter would play her flute or violin, and I would play the piano. We also had a drum player and a guy from the singles group who played the guitar. Our praise and worship team had a grand time practicing together and playing together, especially on Wednesday evenings during the church service.

On Sunday mornings, the praise and worship team sensed another kind of spirit in the atmosphere. It was a critical spirit that was sensed by the majority of us. There were six of us in the praise and worship team.

There was this middle-aged woman who attended this church, who had a spirit of lust about her. She would swoop herself all around the men in the church who were single. She herself was single at the time and the mother of three young children. Shortly after we changed churches, the church had a big division among the members. We stayed long enough to elect a new pastor to minister the flock of people, and then we started going to the Word of Life Church.

It was while we were at the AOG church in that bigger town that I called up the pastor from the church we had attended in Madison and told him that I forgave him for the blunder that he made right before we left that church. He was arrogant and prideful in his response to my forgiveness. He basically told me that he had done nothing wrong. I sent him a book that was written about pastors abusing their authority in the church for him to read. I told God that I was not going to take revenge on the pastor. I was turning him over to God to do what He wanted with him.

> Do not take revenge, my friends, but leave room for God's wrath things for it is written: "It is mine to avenge; I will repay, says the Lord. And you should be busy sowing seed and doing good things for others." (Romans 12:19)

Shortly after this period of time, the rain came to Madison and flooded the pastor's house, and he had to move elsewhere in that town. Also, his wife and he were given the burden and responsibility of raising their grandson who was from the African American culture, and Madison is populated mostly with Caucasians. But maybe he made amends with God because God blessed him and his wife with a new house that they built in the same town. And later, they moved to Sioux Falls, South Dakota.

Some people in the AOG church in that bigger town wondered how my children could be so well kept with my meager wages. I had an organized strategy that worked very well. Each of the children had small jobs that they worked on weekends or part-time during the weekdays. And those wages paid for the desires that the children wanted in life. We all worked hard, helped each other out when one needed help during those days. I worked five part-time jobs, including work study at the college. The girls secured babysitting jobs, and Justin secured a weekly newspaper route, and later he did a daily newspaper route. We all worked hard for our money. God sent people across our path to provide for our clothing that we needed. Each of us had someone in our lives who gave us their hand-me-downs for clothing. Most of the clothing were very stylish and beautiful.

Later, Rachael secured a job at one of the pizza places in town. She eventually moved out on her own into a little trailer house two blocks away from where we lived. She met this young girl who shared the rent with her. She then moved to a little house and lived by herself with her Chihuahua, Itsy.

We changed churches from the Assembly of God to the Word of Life Church. At this church, we found much healing for our wounds that still weren't healed completely. The church started a school, and both my other daughter and Justin were able to attend the school. Someone in the church paid for the tuition for them to attend the school. I volunteered a few hours a week to tutor some of the younger children with their math and reading. The children were taught by loving, godly people the fundamentals of the scholar life that they needed.

We were only at the church about five months when this middle-aged man, Will, walked into the church on a Wednesday night. I was working on my own issues in life after my divorce and the abuse that had taken place in my life. So I just casually looked over at that man and sensed that he was really hurting emotionally the way he was carrying on a conversation with Pastor P. Later I learned that I was right. His wife had just left him, and he was probably heading for a divorce with her. He looked sad and disheartened from the load that he was carrying at that time.

During the years when I was single, I worked on my own baggage that contained the remnants of the abuse that I had experienced from my second marriage. There were many aspects to my life I had to consider when I was raising my children by myself. I was kept very busy with living for the Lord. I wavered whether I even wanted to get married again or whether I just wanted to enjoy my girlfriends and otherwise live alone. I wanted to give my children a chance to experience life without the abuse that they had experienced also. We spent the weekends in the winter going to the hills in the park that was located at the edge of that bigger town and sledding. We would bundle up in our parka coats with the hoods on them, mittens, scarves around our necks, snow boots on our feet and spend hours out in the cold weather, sledding down the hill by the lake. We would go back home and drink hot chocolate and eat homemade cookies or cinnamon rolls and enjoy the warmth of the house.

In the summertime, we would go to Lake Mitchell and swim with our blow-up float pads. We would spend hours in the sun. Sometimes we would take the kids' friends along with us. The weather was hot, so we had to have cold drinks to keep us cool on the inside.

In September 1992, I went to college at DWU in that bigger town. Before I graduated, I worked my internship jobs at various facilities. One of them was a locked-down facility for young adults who were in terrible trouble with the law. While I worked there, I learned the responsibilities of becoming a drug and alcohol abuse counselor.

I also worked in a facility that helped children who had been abused/neglected. Their ages were also eleven to eighteen years old. I worked the overnight shift. About a year later, I was promoted to a daytime shift, where I became a supervisor of a pod of six girls. I worked five days a week, got off Wednesdays, and worked ten hours on Saturdays. On Wednesdays, I would go into the facility and plan the activities that my pod would be participating in for that week. Once a week we, I and the other pod supervisor, would go to the Catholic Church on a Saturday night. My girls would always be on their best behavior, unlike Judy's girls, who acted out on the way to church. I usually drove the twelve-passenger van. We would end up turning around to take those girls back to the facility. We would continue going to church with my girls. One time, Judy asked me, "Why don't your girls act out?"

I replied, "Because I don't treat them like I'm their friend. They have respect for me because I act like a leader instead."

Once a week, on a Saturday, I would go to the Salvation Army store, where my girls would help the manager hang up clothes on Z racks, clean the store, and organize the items in the store. They would get the opportunity to pick out clothes that they wanted for free at the end of the day.

My pod would also go on Saturdays and do various activities. In the summertime, we would clean up the rodeo grounds after the annual rodeo. We also cleaned up the rocks in the area that the city was planning to make into a baseball diamond. It was a hot weather when we did that project. One of my girls stated to me one day, "Are you sweating, Ms. Reno?"

I replied, "Yes. Why?"

She came back with, "Then I know that you're working." What a funny one she was then!

At a later date, one of the girls who I had worked with called me on the phone at work and wanted to talk to me. It ended up that she wanted to thank me for helping her while she was a client at my workplace. I could tell that she had grown up and had a more mature attitude about her. I rejoiced with God that I had made a difference in her life!

CHAPTER 9

Life with Third Husband—In Love Again

After Will had been coming to church at Word of Life for about eight months, I noticed that he was different from other men that I had observed in the past. I started watching how he interacted with other people and how his temperament was in different situations. I liked what I was observing about him. He seemed to be a wonderful person. And eventually, I knew that God had directed his path to the church for a reason. I really admired him and recognized that I loved him. I heard a phrase that was quoted: "When you find the right person to live with forever, it should be with a person that you cannot live without." It's better than the phrase that says, "You should find a person that you can live with."

Besides Will and I going to the same church, we kept meeting at the post office around 3:30 p.m. every day. Finally, we paused and asked each other what we were doing at the post office at that time of day.

"Why do you come here at this time?"

"I get the mail before I go get the kids from school."

"Why are you here at this time?"

"I get my mail before I go home to sleep since I work at night."

Years later, when I was married to Will, my third husband, I listened to a female evangelist, Joyce Meyers, who told about her childhood and adulthood experiences. She shared about her personal experience with taking Jesus into her heart instead of just giving Him lip service. And He revealed scriptures to her that helped her overcome all the turmoil and restlessness in her life. Once she had made the dedication and commitment to Jesus, she could then stand before Him as a righteous child. She had tried being good and doing good things for others, but not until she got the Word of God into her heart did she start living victoriously.

Some of the scriptures that she learned to believe in were the following:

He who dwells in the secret place shall rest in the shadow of the Almighty. I will say of the Lord, He is my refuge and my fortress my God, in whom I trust. (Psalm 91:1)

Instead of their shame my people will receive portion, and instead of disgrace they will rejoice in their inheritance; and so they will inherit a double portion in their land, and everlasting joy will be theirs. (Isaiah 61:7–8)

Trust in the Lord and do good; dwell in the land and enjoy safe pasture. Delight yourself in the Lord and He will give you the desires of your heart. Commit your way to the Lord; trust in Him and He will do this; He will make your righteousness shine like the dawn, the justice of your cause like the noonday sun. (Psalm 37:3)

Do not take revenge, my friends, but leave room for God's wrath things for it is written: "It is mine to avenge; I will repay, says the Lord. And you should be busy sowing seed and doing good things for others." And this woman of God also said, "But grace also sees when our heart is right towards God and even though our performance may not always be perfect, grace forgives and helps us get from where we are to where we need to be. Grace removes condemnation and sets us free. Free from negative traps and free to serve God without pressure." (Romans 12:19)

During those nine years, when I was single, raising my last two children by myself, I was working five to six part-time jobs, and going to college for a bachelor's degree year-round. I put a lot of trust in God for the many things that were needed. Some of the scriptures that I applied to my life at that time and still do in these days while I walk this earth are the following:

- Psalm 56:1. I put my trust in You God, in whom shall I be afraid. What can man do to me? And I thank Him for being my steadfast God through poverty and famine, through heartache and distraught, through sickness and in health, through depression and happiness/hopefulness, through fatigue and energetic times, and through turmoil and peaceful/refreshing times.
- Isaiah 26:3–4. I trusted in the Lord because He is my rock forever. Beth had the opportunity to come and see me while we lived in that bigger town in South Dakota. I had met her in 1984 while working at the nursing home in Sioux Falls.

  Corrie ten Boom, a Holocaust survivor, stated, "But this is what the past is for! Every experience God gives us, every person He puts in our lives, is the perfect preparation for the future that only He can see."
- Psalm 116:5–9. I was able to relax because I knew and still know that the Lord cares for me. He saved me from death, He stopped my eyes from crying, and He kept me from defeat. I walked with the Lord in the land of the living. I walked free from fear because of my confidence and trust in the Lord. I know that He rewards those that diligently seek Him.

- Hebrews 11:6. But without faith it is impossible to please Him, for he who comes to God must believe that He is, and that He rewards those who diligently seek Him.

Colin had been dating a number of women until he met Becky. In June of 1997, Colin and Becky were married. Their first son, Calin, was born in April of that year. And then Will and I were married in September of that same year. It was a very small wedding with just our dear friends attending. We did take time for a honeymoon to the east coast, Pennsylvania, where Will's biological mother, Theresa, and his siblings live.

And on the way back from our honeymoon, we got the news that Will's adoptive mother had passed away suddenly. As soon as we got back to South Dakota, we repacked our bags and flew out to California to plan the funeral of his dear mother, Anna. We then had the decision to make of whether or not we would sell the house or move to California and live in the house where he grew up. We cleaned out the house and went home to South Dakota to pray on what our decision would be in the end. In May of 1998, we came out to California and painted the inside of the house, cleaned carpets, and dry-cleaned the draperies in the living room.

Will, Justin, and I moved to California in August of 1998, where we settled down into the home that Will's mom and dad had left for Will. Will and I settled into our new lives in California by seeking for employment quickly. We located a temporary job service in order to obtain employment. It seemed that Will would work a temporary job for two weeks, and then he would be unemployed, and I would work for two weeks. This continued until early in 1999, when Will secured a job with a paper-shredding company as a security guard.

Justin didn't settle into his new life very well. He became very paranoid when we left the house and didn't tell him where we were going and what time we would be back home again. We acquired cell phones so we could more readily communicate with him and others. He stayed very rebellious toward Will and me during that time. He didn't understand why he had to move out to California, away from his friends and his older sister, Rachael.

I finally made the decision that Justin would spend some time with his sister Rachael in South Dakota. It wasn't long, and he wasn't getting along with Rachael. This was mainly because Rachael was living on a shoestring. She was barely making it financially the way it was with her income. But she supported Justin in obtaining jobs and enrolled him in the high school where she was living. She even let him drive her car in order to get to and from his jobs.

Eventually, I received a phone call from Trent, asking me, "So is it all right for Justin to stay with me?"

I told him, "Yes, just for a little while."

The intention of sending Justin to South Dakota, on my part, was to let him learn more about how cantankerous Trent really was as a person. Justin had these thoughts and ideas about Trent that he was a better person than what he really was in character. The intention of sending him to stay with Rachael was never for Justin to stay living in South Dakota. I was his legal guardian, and he was a minor yet. Eventually, I got another phone call from Trent, asking, "Should I send Justin back to California?"

I replied to that question with, "Of course you should. He's my son. I love him, and he needs to live with Will and me as his parents!"

When Justin returned to California, he was still a very mixed-up teenager. He was still full of rage from what had happened to him in his younger years. The treatment that his own dad gave him was not that as a loving, protective parent but quite the opposite. He started having suicidal ideas and tendencies. We quickly got counseling through a behavioral mental health center close to our home, and all three of us went for counseling. Through outpatient counseling sessions that we attended, we learned distinctive factors about one another and ourselves.

Justin attended the Christian high school for one year and dropped out of school at the age of eighteen. He studied and tested for his graduate education diploma and passed that to complete his educational program. Years later, he worked for and obtained a bachelor's degree in business administration. This degree has helped him to secure other job positions.

In June of 1999, I had arthroscopy surgery on my left knee for a torn meniscus. I was recovering from surgery when we accepted the foreign exchange students into our home. I had secured a job with a Xerox project through the temporary job service. From there, I obtained a permanent job working for Edison Security Alarm Systems located in San Dimas, California. This happened right after we accepted the foreign exchange students in our home.

While Justin was gone, I got empty nest syndrome. So Will and I decided to have a foreign exchange student come live with us. Her name was Hoi K Cheuk, otherwise known as Carly, and she was from Hong Kong. After a couple of weeks, we were asked if we wanted to have another foreign exchange student from Japan to stay with us. Her sponsors were unable to keep her because of a family crisis in their home. We conferred with Carly. She consented to have Marie Tamisuto join our home. They lived with us for the school year, then they returned home and took a test to see if they passed. Afterward, they were able to attend college, either in their home country or abroad. Carly's sister was attending college in Australia, and she joined her the following year. Carly earned two bachelor of arts degrees (one in business accounting and one in social economics) from the university in Australia. Marie returned to the US and attended a university in San Francisco, California. She became a translator after graduating from college. Marie's second languages were French and English.

Our daughter, Mackenzie, returned home from serving at a boot-camp type of ministry in Texas. She worked for a women's shelter during her stay at home. Carly and she became very close; they shared various similarities, such as they both loved to play the flute and piano, they both liked to sing, and they were very close in age. Carly was seventeen when she lived with us. Carly would attend the youth group on Wednesday nights. Carly was led to the Lord by the youth group of Pastor Bob at the end of her stay with us. She was given a couple of Bibles to take home with her, and she was very happy about the decision that she made for her life.

Mackenzie returned to Dallas, Texas, for Bible college in 2000. While she was completing her studies there, she met her future husband. Will and I flew out to Texas that year to meet and spend some time with them. In December 2001, they were married in a Jewish ceremony. It was a very festive occasion, and much celebration was done. What a joyful event that was for all of us! Rachael also went down for the wedding.

Another important turning point in my life started with my continuing college experience. September 2001, I started college to earn a master's degree in education guidance counseling. I finished that degree and graduated in December 2004. I met Dr. Marge in the last quarter of that master's degree, and she encouraged me to start the master's program in vocational rehabilitation counseling.

It was in this period of time that I decided to host a Pampered Chef party at our house. The Pampered Chef guy, whom I bought the items from, came to our house ahead of time of the party. He and I prepared the food with the items that he provided for the party. He and I were laughing and having a grand old time fixing the food. At one point, he stated to me, "Why do you laugh at my jokes? Do you really think that they are funny?"

I replied, "Yes, they are clean jokes, and I think that they are hilarious!"

So we proceeded with the party.

I bought several items from Pampered Chef, and afterward, they were delivered to my house. I had a question about a couple of items that I received, so I called the guy, Mike, on the phone. I knew his brother, who was a pastor, and his wife, and they had told me that they never could get Mike to make a personal commitment to Jesus in his life. While I had Mike on the phone, I asked him what his reason was for not making a commitment to Jesus. He waited a little while, and then he said to me, "What if I flub up and make a mistake, what will happen to me?"

I replied, "There's a scripture in the Bible that says, if we make mistakes while we are or are not Jesus's children, we are to go to Him and tell Him that we are sorry, and we want Him to forgive us of whatever we have done or said. And He is faithful to forgive us of that very thing."

He let out a sigh and said, "Oh, that doesn't seem so complicated."

I said, "Well, it's not that complicated. So do you want to pray a prayer with me to accept Jesus in your heart?"

He said, "Yes!"

After we had prayed together, I told him to tell his mother, brother, and his wife what he had just done.

The next day was Sunday. We went to the same church as Mike's brother and his wife. They called me up in front of the church to tell how I had led their brother to Jesus. I made it a simple testimony, which it had been a simple thing to accomplish. It was a wonderful experience!

About the time I was in my second year of the first master's degree, Rachael was experiencing some tests and trials in her life. We made a trip back to South Dakota and moved her out to California to help her get back her financial stability. She stayed back in Nebraska with her grandparents until after their anniversary celebration and then flew to California, while she lived with us and worked at Kmart as a cashier and stock person. In 2004, she moved to Northern Nebraska, where she joined the young man, Jess, with whom she had been in contact with the year before she moved out to California. They got married before the justice of the peace in December 2004 and then had an official wedding celebration in July 2005. We flew back for the wedding celebration and met our new grandson, Dillon. He was only four months old at the time. He was a happy baby, and everyone at the wedding wanted to hold him. But it was a very hot day. The temperatures hit 103 degrees that day, with the humidity added onto the heat of the day. So as a protective grandmother, I shooed people away from the baby to allow him to sleep and be free from the grasps of people on that sultry hot day.

I started the master's program in vocational rehabilitation counseling in January 2005 and graduated in December 2006. I found employment serving people with disabilities in the setting of a vendor, Goodwill Southern California, who acted as a catalyst in finding employment for those people. I worked there from October 2007 to September 2009. For the first year, I was a rehabilitation specialist for the supported employment clients with disabilities. I flourished in this position as I carried out all the details/credentials concerning the job description. But I didn't realize that people who worked closely with me were very envious of my skills and abilities to carry out the job position that I held. And with the economic hardship that hit companies, I could replace by giving extra duties another person in management, who had their hands full with the multiple tasks already given to them.

Then after my wages and hours were cut, I was placed in a position that I had managed for the first year I was with the company. When I was placed in a step-down position at the jobsite, I eventually changed my attitude toward the floating job coach position that I was placed in at that time. It was hard at first to work in the step-down position because I was so overqualified for the job. When I started doing my job duties unto the Lord, I decided to be the best floating job coach for the clients that I possibly could be. I prayed diligently for the Lord to deliver me from that job position. I literally filled a spiral notebook full of scriptures that I took to heart at that time and prayers that I prayed. Shortly after that, I was delivered from working for the company. I put in my resignation letter to my supervisors. I received unemployment compensation for a year. After that year was over, Goodwill decided to have a hearing with an unemployment officer. After showing him the spreadsheet that I had prepared, showing the financial hardship that I went through, he granted me another six months of unemployment. I was elated with the results!

On November 21, 2010, I heard Charles Stanley, a television preacher, talk about this very same subject during his television broadcast. He talked about how we should not lead a life like Barnabas of the Bible did. Every time something got too difficult for him, he would bail out and run away from that difficult thing in his life. A person has to focus on the loving Heavenly Father, who is always present, ever powerful, and willing to be of assistance to you. Your faith will fail you if you lose your focus on life. Colossians 3:1 quotes, "If then you were raised with Christ, seek those things which are above, where Christ is, sitting at the right hand of God. Set your mind on things above, not on things on the earth. For you died, and your life is hidden with Christ in God. When Christ, who is our life appears, then you also will appear with Him in glory."

In October of 2010, I had my left knee totally replaced. It was something that needed to be done for over eleven years. I knew that it would be a painful experience, but it would heal in God's time. While I recuperated from the surgery, I had plenty of time to think about life in general. I found a lot of good things to think about in a little book called *God Always Has a Plan B* written by the women Luci Swindoll, Barbara Johnson, Kathy Troccoli, Patsy Clairmont, and Marilyn Meberg, who are known as the Women of Faith ministries. There was a short story in that book that really influenced my life; it was about an English fisherman named Sir Edmond Lancier, who was one of England's foremost painters of wildlife. This short story was written by Barbara Johnson.

An English fisherman went into an inn at the end of the long, cold day and ordered a pot of tea. Bragging to friends about his big catch of fish, he stretched out his arm with a sweeping motion. In an instant he knocked the teapot off the table and against the wall. A dark stain splashed across the wallpaper.

The fisherman was aghast at what he had done and apologized profusely to the innkeeper. He tried to wipe off the tea, but already it had made an ugly blotch. Shortly, a man seated at the next table came up and said, "Calm yourself, Sir." The stranger took out a coal pencil and began to sketch around the shape of the stain. In moments, he created a picture of a majestic stag that looked as if it had been designed for that wall. Soon he was recognized as Sir Edmond Lancier, England's foremost painter of wildlife.

What Sir Edmond Lancier did with an unsightly tea stain in a fine English inn, our God is doing every day. He is working in the lives of people who wonder how they'll ever recover from the ugly things that have happened to them. He

is making masterpieces of our lives that stand
as testimonies to his love and power. (Barbara
Johnson)

Isn't that just beautifully illustrated! Along with the story, there are quoted three scripture verses that gave me extra hope that I needed that day, October 10, 2010.

The ransomed of the Lord will return.
They will enter Zion with singing;
Everlasting joy will crown their heads.
Gladness and joy will overtake them,
And sorrow and sighing will flee away. (Isaiah
35:10)

Let the morning bring me word of your unfailing
love,
For I have put my trust in you.
Show me the way I should go,
For onto you I lift up my soul. (Psalm 143:8)

Be still, and know that I am God. (Psalm 46:10)

Before surgery, I joined an aqua aerobics class, where I worked out and met a lot of wonderful elderly people. When I had to go out for my surgery, they kept in touch with me. Two of them brought me flowers. And then after I was recuperating from the surgery, I had the opportunity to visit with one of the older gals, Joan, who was from England originally. She was a delightful person, who did oil paintings (still life) of the poppy fields she had seen in England. She served me hot tea with milk and sugar in it and her famous sugar cake (fruit cake) that she had made for the Christmas holidays. Every year, she makes sugar cakes for people and, I imagine, gets a little something in cash for making them for people who she knows. Since we are both from European countries, me from Germany and she from England, we have a few things in common with one another.

Through therapy, after my knee surgery, I met many wonderful and interesting people. My therapists have agreed to have their picture taken with me, and I have their permission to include it in this book. Tuffairy Goddess and Ben Sherry were very effective therapists, who brought me through the experience with much encouragement and challenges. After three months of extensive therapy, I was ready to move onto going back to aqua aerobics. I have goals set for my life to accomplish full recovery of my knee. Without goals, I believe that a person just wanders through life without purpose.

Throughout the years, my mom always talked about her childhood friends. And even as an adult, she continued to repeat those stories about Ella, Irene, Sally (my mom's sister), and Charlie, who provided transportation for them. When we moved to California, my mother, Emma, told me that her childhood girlfriend lived out in that state. She also had talked about Ella throughout my adult years and how Ella named me after her sister Irene's daughter, Janice. My mom thought that was such a pretty name, a popular name for that era, and she added the middle name of Ann to Janice for my name. She encouraged me to locate Ella and spend time with her. Since we moved out to California, I did locate and visit with my mother's childhood girlfriend Ella Bell-Lipps-Mederiros. Will, Justin, and I traveled down to Beverly Hills, where she and her late husband, Frank, lived. We visited them three times in the twelve years that we have lived out in California.

The last time that we visited Ella, she told stories about her life with being a friend to my mother, Emma. She told about how she and her sister, Irene, and my mother, Emma, and her sister, Sally, used to chum around together. Ella's younger brother, Carroll, used to run around with these young girls too. I remember my mother, Emma, talking about Carroll Zybach when she talked about Ella. They all lived and grew up around rural Columbus, Nebraska. Before they were married, according to Ella's stories, they would look for guys who they thought that they liked and flirted with them.

Eventually, all four of the young women married. Ella married Jon, Emma married Helmer, Sally married Richard, and Irene married a man with the last name of Strong. Sally lived in Omaha, and

Irene lived in Columbus and owned and operated a doughnut shop. After Ella and Emma were married, they would visit each other at their homes and play cards in the evenings. At that time, my parents lived by Platte Center, located near Columbus. At Christmastime, Ella's husband, Jon, would play Santa Claus for the young kids in those families.

In 1953, Ella, her husband, Jon, and their son, Johnny, moved to Hemet, California, where they resided, until Jon died suddenly of a heart attack. They had adopted Johnny in 1943 as a baby, and their daughter Ruby Ann was adopted in 1955 as a baby.

We had a great time together, and we thought that we would see each other again, but that was not going to be the scenario that took place. Since then, I tried to locate Ella in November 2010. I discovered that both she and Frank had passed away.

I received an invitation to Ella's memorial service, which was held in December 2010. We attended her memorial service, and I met her adopted son, Johnny, and her adopted daughter, Ruby Ann. I also met her niece, Marge Ann, who was her sister Irene's daughter. Ella's granddaughters and two little great grandsons were also at the memorial service. It was wonderful meeting everyone, but I really bonded with Marge Ann, who lives with her son close by her.

After a couple of weeks went by, I contacted Marge Ann and had a very fruitful conversation with her. She helped fill in the gaps of what events took place when the girls, Ella and Emma, were growing up in their childhood. Because we are both interested in other people's lives, this information is important to us. And I believe that my children should know who these people were because they brought joy into the life of my mother, Emma. And they are still bringing joy into my life. Both Marge and I agreed that one era had come to an end. She and I will try to create another era by visiting with one another on the phone and through letter writing. Later on, we might visit one another in person at each other's houses.

What is next in life is what we let God make of it, submitting our lives to Him for guidance and discernment in making decisions that need to be made in our lives. Or we can try to do things in our own stead and see what mistakes we will make of life's decisions.

God's blessing will not be withheld in this coming year, which shall be a year of blessing to those who have been faithful. "So, my faithful ones, get ready for the manifestation of multiple blessings that are coming into your lives. Even though the world itself will be in disarray, even though the economic conditions of this world are not good, you will live within the confines of my blessings. Lift up your heads and let your worship ascend," says the Lord God Almighty. "The glory of God will bring His blessings."

We were praying that 2011 would be what the prophets Marsha and Bill Burns said it would be, "Heaven in eleven." They also prophesied "that the Lord, in His glory, will visit His people in 2011. Our part in this visitation must be the same as that which David spoke of. Psalm 26:6–8: 'I will wash my hands in innocence; so I will go about Your altar, O Lord, that I may proclaim with the voice of thanksgiving, and tell of all Your wondrous works. Lord, I have loved the habitation of Your house, and the place where Your glory dwells.'"

The reason that I even mention this prophecy in my book is because of its accuracy in prophesying what is in the future. I have been receiving this prophecy by email for at least five years, and it has been accurate from the very beginning. It's a prophecy that comes from God, not from a horoscope or tarot cards, which do not originate from God but from God who knows the future of everyone living on this earth because He has created each one of us.

❀

CHAPTER 10

Recession in the United States

In 2009, the recession was raging throughout California and throughout the United States. It seems that when the USA is in war for long periods of time that the country suffers because of it. There are other factors that add to the whole breakdown of the United States. For the past number of years, California has been the state that has taken the brunt of the immigration of people from Mexico, Asian countries, and different countries, such as the islands. All, I believe, contributes to the downfall of our economy and employment opportunities. Businesses are looking for more economic ways of maintaining their establishments, and the rest of us who were here first in the state of California are paying for their decisions.

Will's trucking business, where he had been working for three years prior to 2009, could not make it anymore and therefore closed its doors to business. More and more businesses are cutting back and expecting their workers to multitask and settle for lesser job positions that don't require the skills that degrees call for and lesser pay.

Many people are experiencing the hardship of losing their homes to the banks because of loss of jobs and not being able to pay the high mortgage payments required to keep their home. Bankruptcy attorneys cannot keep up with the load of people who are being forced to file bankruptcy in order to get from underneath the financial load.

But in the spiritual realm of how the country was in 2011, we must put our trust in God, in whom shall we be afraid. What can man do to us? Always thank our steadfast God for His provision, through poverty and famine, through heartache and distraught, through unemployment and employment, through sickness and in health, through depression and happiness/hopefulness, through fatigue and energetic times, through turmoil and peaceful/refreshing times. We must trust in the Lord because He is our rock, our refuge forever. Psalm 116:5–9 says "that I will relax because the Lord cares of me. He saved me from death, He stopped my eyes from crying, and He has kept me from defeat. I walk with the Lord in the land of the living. I walk free from fear because of my confidence and trust in the Lord. I know that He is the reward giver of those that diligently seek Him." Hebrews 11:6 states, "But without faith it is impossible to please Him, for he who comes to God must believe that He is, and that He is a reward giver of those who diligently seek Him."

Daniel, chapter 3, tells about how the God of Shadrach, Meshach, and Abednego protected them in the fiery furnace when Nebuchadnezzar threw them into the furnace because they would not bow down to the gods and worship the gold image, which was set up by man. Nebuchadnezzar saw with his own eyes that there were not three men in the furnace, but there was a fourth man, who he recognized as the Son of God. The three men were able to walk out of the furnace without a hair singed on their heads. Their clothes did not smell of fire or smoke, and they were well. They had a loyalty to God, and they were rewarded for their bravery.

The point is through this biblical story that God Almighty is with each one of us through all of the trials and tribulations. He wants most of all that each person who He has created to have the character of Jesus Christ. Obedience to Him is better than any sacrifice that we can perform. He will pour out His blessings to whoever believes in Him and trusts in Him for their daily sustenance. How can a person have faith in God or obey God when they do not want to believe in Him or accept that He exists and even accept Him as their personal Savior? That person cannot obey someone they don't believe exists. It says in Deuteronomy 28:1–14 that God has promised blessings for obedience.

> Now it shall come to pass, if you diligently obey the voice of the Lord your God, to observe carefully all His commandments which I command you today, the Lord your God will set you high above all nations of the earth. His blessing will overtake you, you will be blessed wherever you go, the fruit of your body will be blessed, all that you own will be blessed, you shall be blessed when you come in, and when you go out. The Lord will cause your enemies who rise against you to be defeated before your face; they shall come out against you one way and flee before you seven ways.

In Genesis 27, Jacob gained Esau's blessing through deception and greediness. Esau gave up his inheritance for a bowl of soup. Esau did not have great regard for his inheritance, otherwise he would not have given it up so easily. But later, he realized what he had done. Jacob felt guilty afterward and tried to make up for his deception with Esau by giving him cattle and parts of his herd. Jacob was the one who wrestled with an angel of God and walked away with a limp because the hip that was shorter than the other was due to his hip being taken out of its socket and the muscle shrank. God changed Jacob's name after that to Israel because he had struggled with God and with men and had prevailed. What is your inheritance? Would you give up your inheritance for a lump sum of money or for things of this world?

We, as true Christians, need to express what we want in life through the words in the Bible. Instead of negative comments and ideas in our mind, we need to renew our minds in Christ Jesus. Psalm 34:1–4 states, "I will bless the Lord at all times; His praise shall continually be in my mouth. My soul shall make its boast in the Lord; the humble shall hear of it and be glad. Oh, magnify the Lord with me, and let us exalt His name together." Joel Osteen has stated that if we make a list of the positive things and negative things in our life, the positive things will outweigh the negative things. And we need to be mindful that what we allow to flow out of our mouths will come to pass in our lives. Psalm 90:17 states, "And let the beauty of the Lord our God be upon us, And establish the work of our hands for us; Yes, establish the work of our hands." Don't wait until Thanksgiving to be thankful; don't wait until Christmas to give gifts. As a person is led to be generous, that's when they are to give to other people.

If you don't like where you are, reinvent who you are. Look up scriptures in the Bible that tell you who you are in Christ. Some of you need to start believing what God says in His Word of who you are in Him. The mind is always the battlefield, as Joyce Meyers says repeatedly in her conferences and on her television programs. The thief/devil does not come except to steal and to kill and to destroy. I/Jesus have come that we may have life, and that we may have it more abundantly. But we can put our trust in God, who reassures us that we Christians have the power, in Jesus's name, to cast the devil out of the situations in our lives here on earth. With such a resource available to us, why should we continue to walk through our lives doing without and putting up with sicknesses and every other evil vice that comes against us?

It is a must for us to cast all of our cares on God and to trust in the Lord with all of our heart and lean not on our own understanding. In all our ways, acknowledge Him, and He shall direct our paths. This is how my family and I got through all of the trials and tribulations in our lives throughout the years. The year 2011 had not been an easy year to get through. We had many trials and tribulations, and we have gained much wisdom, discernment, and revelation from God through it all. When we got knowledge that we should take Jesus into our hearts and acknowledge that He is in control of our lives, then we were given a hope and a future for good and not for evil. Jeremiah 29:11–14 says, "For I know the thoughts that I think toward you, says the Lord, thoughts of peace and not of evil, to give you a future and a hope. Then you will call upon Me and go and pray to Me, and I will listen to you, and you will seek Me and find me, when you search for Me with all your heart, I will be found by you, says the Lord, and I will bring you back from your captivity; I will gather you from all nations and from all the places where I have driven you, says the Lord, and I will bring you to the place from which I cause you to be carried away captive."

I don't know what we would have done without God/Jesus in our lives to lead and guide us through the rough times during our past years of living our lives. The seen and unseen blessings that God/Jesus has bestowed upon us throughout the years are surmountable. I desire to leave a godly legacy for my children, grandchildren, and great-grandchildren. But my fear is that they won't catch onto the truth about the spiritual portion of their lives and the lives of their past relatives. I pray that the Holy Spirit will visit each one of my loved ones and friends, showing them the truth about God/Jesus.

I want to leave you all with this last provoking thought from John C. Maxwell's book that teaches about the leadership that lies within each one of us; it also can pertain to our attitude toward life in general.

We cannot choose how many years we will live, but we can choose how much life those years will have.

We cannot control the beauty of our face, but we can control the expression on it.

We cannot control life's difficult moments, but we can choose to make life less difficult.

We cannot control the negative atmosphere of the world, but we can control the atmosphere of our minds.

Too often, we try to choose to control things we cannot.

Too seldom, we choose to control what we can…our attitude.

And what we cannot control in life, we have to give up to God/Jesus and let Him take over where we have no concept of what will happen next in life.

CHAPTER II

Lives of Our Grown Children, Grandchildren; the Birth of Our Great-Grandchildren

Let's go back a few years in order to catch up with the when and wheres of our four children, our nine grandchildren, and our two great grandchildren.

When Will and I were married on September 19, 1997, we already had four children, Colin, Rachael, Mackenzie, and Justin. Colin and his wife, Becky, already had their oldest son, Calin. When Will married me, he became a husband, father of four, and a grandfather of one child. A year later Calin had a brother, Jabe, born to the family.

In 2020, Calin and his wife, Hailey, had a little girl, Alice. In 2022, they had another little girl named Emily.

Rachael married Jess, and they had three children: Dillon, Ben, and Lynette. Jess and Rachael got a divorce, and she moved back to South Dakota from Nebraska to raise her three children by herself. In the meantime, Will and I moved back to South Dakota after living in California for twenty-three years to help with the raising of these three children. Since then, Rachael has met a wonderful, God-fearing man; they plan on getting married soon, maybe even this year.

Our second daughter, Mackenzie, is married to Mark. They have four lovely children.

Justin stayed out in California to live with his spouse. He has a BA in business administration and had certification as a CNA.

REFERENCES

Burns, M. and B. Burns. "The Spirit of Prophecy Bulletin." January 2011.

Friel, Linda and John Friel. *Adult Children: The Secrets of Dysfunctional Families*. 1988.

Hoover, Edgar J. "The Biography Channel." Retrieved October 28, 2013. Picture, 08:45. http://www.biography.com/people/j.edgar-hoover-9343398.

Johnson, Barbara. *God Always Has a Plan B*. Grand Rapids, Michigan: The Zondervan Corporation, 1999, 76.

Kennedy John F. "The Biography Channel." Retrieved October 28, 2013, 08:47. http://www.biography.com/people/johnf.kennedy.

Maxwell, John C. *Developing the Leader within You*. Nashville, Tennessee, 1993.

Meyer, Joyce. *Battlefield of the Mind*, Fenton, Missouri, 1995.

Osteen, Joel. *It's Your Time Now*. York, NY, November 2009.

Roosevelt, Franklin D. "The Biography Channel." Retrieved October 28, 2013. Picture, 08:46. http://www.biography.com/people/franklind.roosevelt.

Sherrill, John, Elizabeth Sherrill, and Corrie ten Boom. *The Hiding Place*.

Stanley, Charles. *In Touch with God*. November 21, 2010.

The Open Bible Expanded Edition: The New King James Version Red Letter Edition. 1985, 1983.

The Word in Life Bible. Thomas Nelson. Nashville-Camden-New York. Copyright 1993, 1996, 1998.

ABOUT THE AUTHOR

Janice has the ability and knowledge to express and expound on various events and situations in her life. She was raised as a child and young adult in the country. Later in life, she adapted to living in suburban areas of at least four different states in the United States. She has had more than enough education to help her with writing skills. And thus, she expresses herself with the true feelings she has about the events in her past and present life that have taken place, both good and bad.

Janice A. Yehnert
Education and Credentials

Master of Arts in Rehabilitation Counseling
California State University, San Bernardino, California

Master of Science in Educational Counseling Guidance
California State University, San Bernardino, California

Bachelors of Arts in Human Services/Minor in Criminal Justice
Dakota Wesleyan University, Mitchell, South Dakota

Certified Vocational Rehabilitation Counselor (CRCC)

Certificate of Completion Award—Navigator Training Series

California Clear Pupil Personnel Services Credential (PPS)